This book is dedicated to
Linda Easterling Aycock
(1947–2014)

The wife of my best friend. She loved her family, God, teaching,
the University of Texas Longhorns, the Republican Party, and Tab.
Linda was a gifted editor. And an even better friend.

The Pot Thief
Who Studied
Georgia O'Keeffe

Prologue

I thought black helicopters were an urban myth. Like alligators in the New York City sewers or a tooth dissolving overnight in a glass of Coke.

But the swooshing behind me was not a thrashing gator or a foaming glass of cola. It came from the rotors of a machine with opaque windows and no markings.

It was slowing to land but still gaining on me, in part because I didn't have the good sense not to look back. It's hard to run with your neck swiveled past your shoulder.

I reached the slot between the boulders just as sand from the copter's landing obscured the landscape. That was good. They couldn't see which way I turned after clearing the gap.

The cliff dwelling was to the right. I clambered up to it, hid behind the blue grama grass and stared at the gap between the boulders. *Maybe the only guy in there is the pilot. He's not going to leave the machine and start out on foot,* I said to myself.

Fat chance, my self answered back.

Two guys in desert camouflage came through the slot carrying automatic weapons. The first word that sprung to mind was *Guantánamo.*

The next one was *waterboarding.*

I don't pay much attention to current events, so I'm not exactly sure what waterboarding is. But I'm pretty certain it's not a beach sport.

I'm not a terrorist, just a harmless pot thief.

No, not that kind of pot. The clay kind. Specifically, pots made by New Mexico's ancient pueblo dwellers. Neither the National Security Agency, the Central Intelligence Agency nor the Defense Intelligence Agency is charged with stopping pot thieves. That duty falls to the Bureau of Land Management, and I didn't think the BLM would send me to Guantánamo.

But would the guys in the black helicopter buy my story that I was just digging up artifacts? Or would they assume that since I had breached one of the securest sites in the country, the digging was just a cover for espionage? After all, it was the third time I'd gained unauthorized entry.

The camo guys split up after they cleared the passage between the boulders. I relaxed a bit when the one who came my way sprinted past my perch.

But he stopped after fifty yards. He had seen me run, so he probably figured if he couldn't catch up with me after fifty yards, I had sought cover, a commodity of which there is precious little in the desert.

He scanned the terrain with binoculars. When he didn't spot anything at ground level, he aimed the glasses at the mountain-side. Sunlight glinted off the lenses. I held my breath and put my faith in the Tompiro people who built the cliff dwelling and the grama grass that shielded its entrance.

1

⁓

The first thing I noticed about Carl Wilkes when he walked into Spirits in Clay was his beard had grown back after the chemo. It was neatly trimmed as it had been before the melanoma, but it was now mostly gray.

"You look a lot better than you did the last time I saw you."

"People who've been dead for a year look better than I did then."

"The important thing is you beat it."

"Yeah, Leon Spinks beat Muhammad Ali, but did you see Leon's face after the fight? You still make bad coffee?"

I gave him a cup. He looked around as he sipped. "I don't see that Tompiro pot. You sell it?"

"Last year."

"Get the thirty thousand you had it priced at?"

I nodded.

"You don't seem very happy about it."

"I had it almost twenty years. Now it's gone."

He was silent for a moment. "It was ugly."

I laughed. "Yeah, it was. That's the way they made them. I'll bet the potter thought it was beautiful. And I think it had a kind of inner beauty, imparted from its maker. I miss it."

"If you liked it so much, why did you sell it?"

"I had a buyer. I miss every pot I've ever sold. But I'm a dealer, not a collector. If I'm not willing to sell the pots, I should close the shop."

I poured myself some coffee. It wasn't all that bad.

He looked at me with those deep-set eyes. "There's something else, isn't there?"

"This place is just a way station for pots. I rescue them from the earth, pass them on to collectors who appreciate them."

"What if you didn't see it that way? What if, instead of pots, you were digging up gold nuggets, something natural that you couldn't connect to any human hand?"

Carl's cynical streak is tempered by his humor.

"I have no interest in gold. I don't dig up pots for the money. Like the mountain climber, I dig them up because they're there. Because people who walked this land centuries before I was born made them. It seems sacrilegious to just leave them there, never to be seen again."

"You may dig them up because you don't like the idea of them spending eternity in the dirt, but you make big bucks in the process."

"The money is a nice bonus. But the money from the Tompiro is already gone. The pleasure of unearthing it never will be."

"You need to experience that pleasure again. I have a buyer."

"You had a buyer for that Mogollon pot I stole from the museum, but his money disappeared when I finally got the pot."

"This buyer is legit. Prominent citizen. Tons of money."

"Even so, Tompiro pots are hard to come by."

He nodded. "That's why I came to you."

Wilkes launched me into a life of crime five years ago with

an offer of $25,000 to steal a pot from a museum. Even though he enticed me, I can't blame the museum caper on Carl. But I also don't think it was entirely my fault. I admit my moral fiber unraveled enough to allow me to consider it. A reconnoiter of the museum brought me to my senses, and I decided not to do it.

But the moment I got home, a federal agent accused me of the very crime I had just resisted. I thought maybe that was a sign I ought to do it. If you're going to be punished anyway, why not commit the crime?

The pot in question—a spectacular Mogollon water jug— ended up in my possession but was eventually returned to the museum. I will not add the words *where it belonged*. That pot is all that remains of the life of the woman who made it. She put part of her soul in that clay. It deserves to be held and cherished by someone who cares. It does not belong on a plinth behind velvet ropes in a room no one ever visits.

Carl's second foray into my otherwise placid life did not involve any illegalities, just a blindfolded ride to an unknown location to do a simple appraisal of a collection of ancient pots. Which led to two murders, both of which I was charged with.

You may be wondering why, given my experiences with Carl, I fell for his latest get-rich-quick opportunity.

It's simple—I needed the money.

Of course, I didn't know I would end up in that cliff dwelling.

2

I opened my *Benchmark New Mexico Road & Recreation Atlas* to page seven and plopped it down in front of Susannah. Her margarita had no salt on its rim and was half empty.

"You're late," she said, and looked down at the atlas. Then she smiled and said, "You got lost and had to resort to a map?"

It was a joke, not a question. I could walk the three blocks from my shop to Dos Hermanas Tortillaria while unconscious. Come to think of it, I've made the return trip in that condition a time or two.

We meet there most days at five for chips, salsa and conversation, all of which mix well with tequila, lime juice and triple sec. Not to mention the spectacular New Mexico sunsets above the west mesa and the smell of piñon smoke hanging sweetly in the crisp desert air.

"Sorry. I was studying the atlas and lost track of time. Look at the outline of the state and tell me what shape it has."

She's accustomed to my quirks, so she played along. "It's basically a rectangle."

"You know what I see when I look at it? A doughnut."

"New Mexico has a hole in the middle?"

I nodded.

She asked where the hole was, and her eyes followed my finger as I placed it just south of the middle of the state.

She squinted at the small type. "Trinity Site? The atom bomb blew a hole in the state?"

"Sort of."

"Not a good comparison. The hole in a doughnut goes all the way through. I suppose the bomb made a crater, but you can't look through it and see the sky over China."

She was right, of course. The detonation of the first atom bomb on July 16, 1945, vaporized the tower it was attached to and blasted out a big depression. But not as big as the depression I feel when I think about how many nuclear weapons have been built since then.

"The hole I'm talking about wasn't caused by the explosion. It was caused by the bomb."

"Huh? How can it be caused by the bomb but not the explosion?"

"Because if you're going to explode an atomic bomb, you need lots of space. So the government confiscated over three thousand square miles of land just to blow up one bomb."

"Well they couldn't very well blow it up with people around. And it isn't like the land was scenic oceanfront."

"Some of us think desert landscapes are more scenic than oceanfront. And it was over three thousand square miles. That's larger than Connecticut and Rhode Island combined."

She pointed down at the map. "See these words right next to Trinity Site? *Jornada de Muerto*. If you have to blow up a big bomb, what better placed than one called Journey of Death? Where else could they have done it?"

"I don't know—Detroit?"

She chuckled. "So the hole is just a metaphor?"

"Right. Even if the bomb had been a dud, the hole would still be there. It's called the White Sands Missile Range. It's over a hundred and fifty miles north to south and fifty miles east to west. You can't walk on it. You can't drive through it. You can't even fly over it. It's in the middle of my state like a big doughnut hole and I can't get in."

She stared at me for a few seconds. "Ooooh, I get it. There's a place inside the missile range where you want to steal some pots."

My name is Hubert Schuze, and I've already admitted to you that I'm a pot thief. At least according to the Archaeological Resources Protection Act (ARPA). It's an unjust law, and I've been successfully ignoring it for over twenty years. I've never been caught. I've never even been charged. Although I have to admit that my illegal digging has occasionally plunged me into other sorts of *agua caliente*, but that's just a matter of bad luck.

"It isn't stealing," I said. "I was making a living digging up and selling ancient pots before ARPA was passed. I should have been grandfathered. Making my livelihood illegal after I already started practicing it is unconstitutional."

"Yeah, I remember that from when I was in pre-law. I can't remember what it's called, some phrase like *post office*."

"I think it's *ex post facto*."

She smiled. "Or maybe it's *E pluribus unum*."

"Whatever it's called, it isn't fair. How would you feel if you were a lowly peddler selling brooms door-to-door, and Congress passed a law requiring everyone to buy a vacuum cleaner? You'd be out of business."

"That's a ridiculous example, Hubie. Congress can't make people buy vacuum cleaners."

"They can make you buy health insurance. The Supreme Court said so."

"Health insurance is a far cry from vacuum cleaners."

"Right. Vacuum cleaners are cheap and you use them every day. Health insurance is expensive and you hope you never use it."

Her teasing me about being a thief is a staple of our cocktail-hour banter.

"I know your standard line by heart," she said. "The people who created those pots would prefer to have them admired rather than hidden away in the ground, and they belong to anyone who has the skill to find them."

"And I have that skill. But what good does it do me? I can't get in."

She twirled her glass and smiled at me. "Actually, you can."

I perked up. Susannah has shown considerable pluck as an accomplice in my illegal capers, from kicking in doors to shooting the gun out of a bad guy's hand à la Annie Oakley. Maybe she had a clever plan.

"How can I get in?"

"This is the month they open the Trinity Site to visitors."

I perked back down.

"I already thought of that. It won't work. The gate is open only from eight in the morning until two in the afternoon. So I'd have to drive along in broad daylight and just hope none of the MPs or the two thousand tourists notice me steer off the road and head out across open desert toward the Oscura Mountains and a site I think might contain some Tompiro pots."

"Maybe you could find a turnoff when no cars are close and drive your four-wheel Bronco along a deep arroyo."

"Seems like a long shot."

"You won't know if you don't try. And if it turns out to be impossible to leave the road without being spotted, you could just visit the Trinity Site like the other tourists."

"I don't want to visit the Trinity Site. I want to visit a ruin on the western slope of the Oscura Mountains." I shrugged. "It's irritating that I can't go there. I need the money, but it isn't worth the risk. Although I sometimes think of myself as a short Indiana Jones, the truth is we don't have much in common."

"Yeah. Starting with the fact that you're real and he's a fictional character."

"But he's a *real* fictional character."

"As opposed to what? A *fictional* fictional character?"

"No. I mean he's real in the sense that they created his character with the movies. We all know him. He's tall and daring and frequently swashes his buckle."

"Or buckles his swash. You can also be pretty daring when you have to be."

"But I don't *want* to have to be. I hate taking risks."

"So if it looks too risky, just keep driving until you reach the Trinity Site. It might be interesting."

"It is not interesting. The only facilities are the Porta-Potties next to the parking lot, and the only thing to see besides the big crater are the trinitites."

"That's what they call people who live there?"

"No one lives there, Suze. Trinitites are pieces of the stuff created by the explosion. It was hotter than the surface of the sun and fused the desert sand into glasslike chunks."

"You could bring back a piece as a souvenir."

"Not if I ever want to have children."

"They're radioactive?"

"Yeah, and you're not allowed to touch them. Some of the isotopes in those green chunks have a half-life of twenty-five thousand years."

"Why not just say they have a full life of fifty thousand years?"

"I don't know, and it doesn't matter. There is no prospect of me having children."

"You're not too old to be a father."

"I wasn't referring to my age." I'm between forty and fifty. Okay, closer to fifty.

"Oh. So you and Sharice still haven't—"

"No."

"So what's the holdup?"

Susannah is refreshingly blunt. She's short of thirty the same number of years I am from fifty. She's tall and outdoorsy with thick brown hair and big brown eyes that betray her every mood. She's attractive but not like the contestants in a traditional beauty contest. Which is a good thing, because I can't imagine her consenting to parade around in a bikini. But despite a dazzling smile that matches her personality, she hasn't yet attracted the right guy. Maybe men can't deal with her lack of guile. She's not the person to ask how you look if you happen to be ugly.

I pointed down at the cast on my ankle. "This thing makes it sort of awkward."

A mischievous smile formed on her lips. "Awkward could be fun."

"Not going to happen. She said maybe after the cast is off."

"You had the cast off, and it didn't happen."

"I had it off for one day. Then I had to have a new one on."

"I still can't believe you re-sprained your ankle jumping off the curb."

"It's a higher-than-normal curb."

"Right. Ten inches."

I ignored the sarcasm. "I get this one off tomorrow, but sex with Sharice is still a maybe."

"You've been dating for months. How long does it take the girl to decide she likes a guy enough to—"

"I don't think that's the issue. The *maybe* is not about whether she likes me. It's about something she has to tell me before we have sex."

Now it was her turn to perk up. "You have any idea what this something is?"

"Not a clue."

"Darn. I'm dying to know."

"Not as much as I am. I have more riding on it."

She laughed and said, "Let's try to figure it out."

"I'm not sure I want to discuss—"

"Come on, Hubie. Don't be so uptight. You need to be prepared for whatever it is. If we can think of all the possibilities, you won't be caught off guard. Maybe I can even give you some hints about how a girl might want you to respond."

"Respond to what?"

"To whatever the thing is she has to tell you before you two roll in the hay."

"I just told you I don't know what it is."

"That's why we need to make a complete list. You must have thought about it, so give me the possibilities that came to mind."

She pulled a pencil from her purse, smoothed her napkin on the tabletop and looked at me expectantly.

I was uncomfortable with this discussion, but once Susannah gets the bit between her teeth, she's difficult to whoa.

"Well, one thought I had was maybe she's a . . . uh, that she's never . . ."

She started laughing. "You think she's a virgin?"

"Well, you wanted possibilities."

"You have a picture of her?"

I retrieved the one Sharice had given me and handed it across the table.

Susannah studied the picture. "She's beautiful and exotic, sort of like Carmen Veranda."

"That's Carmen *Miranda*."

She frowned. "Did they name that warning after her?"

"No, her brother," I said deadpan.

She returned the picture to me. "She's attractive, she's in her thirties and we know she dates. She is *not* a virgin."

"She's from Canada." I just sort of blurted it out.

She rolled her eyes. "Just because the weather up there is frigid doesn't mean the women are. What do your lips tell you? Does she kiss like a virgin?"

"So far as I know, the only virgin I ever kissed was Lupita Fuentes."

"Yeah, you told me that story. Your birthday piñata broke open and you and Lupita jumped for the same piece of candy. She grabbed it first, stuck it on her tongue and asked you if you wanted to taste it."

"Which I did. And since she was eleven, it's safe to assume she was a virgin."

"Probably. But the way she was handing out French kisses makes me wonder how long she remained one."

"Can we move on to another possibility?"

"You look so sweet when you're embarrassed. What's next on the list?"

"Maybe she's contemplating becoming a nun."

She threw her hands in the air. "And she's dating you just as a test to see if she'd be able to resist sex the rest of her life?"

"She seems to know a lot about friars."

"How did chickens get into this conversation?"

"Not f-r-y-e-r-s. F-r-i-a-r-s."

"Monks?"

"Right. She told me that in Canada, Carmelites are called White Friars and Dominicans are called Black Friars. Maybe she knows about the orders because she's contemplating entering one."

"Or more likely it's just because she's from Canada and has heard people call them that all her life. Why are they called that, by the way?"

"The Dominicans wear black cloaks and the Carmelites wear white ones."

"Glad we cleared that up. Maybe your chances of having sex with Sharice would improve if you talked about something a bit more romantic than monks."

"She's the one who brought it up."

"Why?"

"She was making a point about black and white."

"She's hesitating to have sex with you because you're white?"

"No. On my last visit to the dentist, she gave me two toothbrushes."

Susannah did that thing where she pulls her shoulders back and thrusts her head forward. It makes her look goofy but still cute, and it means she's confused.

"And you think I'm bad about non sequencers?" she asked.

"That's *non sequiturs*."

"Whatever. I only get one toothbrush from my hygienist."

"So do I. But this time Sharice gave me two, a white one she said was mine and a black one she said I can keep for her at my place just in case."

She smiled at me. "I think we can eliminate the becoming-a-nun theory."

3

Angie showed up to ask if we were ready for a second round. Susannah said we were and ordered refills even though I didn't need one.

"My glass is half full," I said.

"Always the optimist," she replied.

"No, it really is."

"Well, I'm not delaying my second one just because you were late."

I gulped the last of my drink and took the opportunity to change the subject. "So how are things with Baltazar?"

"Fine, but I don't know if our romance will survive the commute."

"Seems like you do most of the driving."

"I work the lunch shift. He works the dinner shift. Easier for me than him."

We met Baltazar Zaragoza in La Reina, a remote village in northern New Mexico where he tends bar at a place with the unlikely name El Eructo del Rey—the King's Belch. Although given the quirkiness of La Reina, maybe the name is appropriate. Susannah and I had gone there in order to find out if a corpse I accidentally dug up was a mummy or a modern person.

Don't ask.

Baltazar is tall, dark and handsome. Susannah used her feminine wiles to wrangle a date with him. I don't know what a *wile* is, but Susannah evidently has lots of them.

"Speaking of Baltazar," she said, and pulled a ripped canvas out of her book bag. She unrolled it onto the table and asked me if I recognized the artist.

An impossibly blue sky shaded down to a cliff of brick-red Chinle sandstone. A rustic farmhouse—adobe walls and tin roof—sat next to a strange cistern.

"There's something odd about that cistern," I said.

"Yeah. It's too large for watering horses and too small for irrigation."

"You would know about that, rancher girl. But what I think is odd is my sense that I've seen it before."

"Given your pot-hunting travels, there are very few things in New Mexico you haven't seen. But forget the cistern. What do you think of the painting?"

"Looks like some unskilled painter trying to imitate Georgia O'Keeffe."

"No, the brushstrokes and the color blending are marks of an accomplished painter. This canvas isn't unskilled—it's merely unfinished."

"I'll take your word for that—you're the art history graduate student. But am I at least right that it looks a bit like O'Keeffe?"

That mischievous grin slithered across her face. "It doesn't just *look* like her. It *is* her."

I examined its frayed edges and dirty surface. "It's not signed. And it looks like it was pulled out of a Dumpster. Why would you think it's an O'Keeffe?"

"For the same reasons you think something is a Tompiro pot—it's what I study. I know her work when I see it."

"Where did you get it?"

"From Baltazar."

"A bartender in La Reina owns an O'Keeffe?"

"He found it a few years ago hiking in the wilderness."

"No wonder it's all beat up. Canvases just aren't suited to wilderness hiking."

"Ha-ha. Baltazar is a friend of the earth. Any trash he sees while hiking, he brings back. When he saw this canvas fluttering in a bush, he thought it was a sack or piece of clothing. He gave it to me after I told him I study art history."

"So instead of a candy wrapper or a cigarette butt, some tourist littered the landscape with a Georgia O'Keeffe canvas?"

"It wasn't a tourist. And she didn't throw it away. It probably blew away, and she couldn't chase it down because she was too old."

"She?"

"Yeah. Georgia O'Keeffe."

"Georgia O'Keeffe was in La Reina?"

"No. Baltazar didn't find it in his village. He was hiking, remember? You have New Mexico's geography almost completely memorized. He found it west of Mogote Ridge. You know where that is?"

The familiar frisson of pot finding made my shoulders twitch. "Yeah. There's a primitive trail, largely unmarked and nearly impassable in places, that leads from Mogote Ridge down to Ghost Ranch."

"Right. And O'Keeffe used to hike up that trail to do plein air painting."

It sounded like her lips briefly stuck together as she pronounced *plain*.

"You mean plain air?"

"No, *plein air*. It's French for plain air."

"So it's the same phrase with the same words and the same meaning except you have to do something weird with your lips to make *plain* sound like *plein*."

"Exactly. We learn lots of important stuff in graduate school."

"How far west was Baltazar from Mogote Ridge?"

"Near the mouth of an arroyo at the base of El Monte Rojo. And that's a place she used to paint."

"That would be Arroyo del Yeso."

I closed my eyes and conjured up United States Geological Survey map 20131206. I didn't know the number—I looked that up later. I'm good, but I'm not *that* good.

The arroyo leads up to the trail that passes Dead End Tank on its way to Mogote Ridge. I let my mind zoom out to a view of north-central New Mexico and realized that if you continue due east and don't fall off the ledge or get attacked by a mountain lion, you'll eventually reach La Reina.

Made sense, except for the ranch house and cistern. Something didn't fit. And I couldn't shake the feeling I'd seen that cistern before.

She rolled the canvas up and returned it to her book bag. "I'm taking this to class tonight so I can ask Dr. Casgrail about it."

4

~

Tristan slid a surgical mask over his nose and mouth and handed one to me.

"Why are we wearing these?" I asked.

"To keep from breathing the plaster dust."

He attached a saw blade the size of a quarter to his Dremel rotary tool. "You sure you want me to do this? It would be easier and safer just to crack it."

"In which case you'd have to use a hammer. I think I'll take my chances with the little saw. Plus, I want to save all the signatures. So cut in between them."

Geronimo trotted in, evidently attracted by the high-pitched whine of the rotary tool. It sounded like a dentist's drill, so I did what I always do when I hear that noise. I closed my eyes and clamped a death grip on the arm of my chair.

The saw buzzed on and off for a while in five-second bursts. When the noise stopped altogether, I opened my eyes and looked down.

"The cast is still on."

"I didn't want to saw all the way through and run the risk of cutting you. So I stopped each time I saw the first hint of gauze."

He removed his mask and took a deep breath. He put one hand on each side of the cast, gave a gentle tug, and it came away easily in two pieces.

"Impressive," I said.

"Aawk," he said, and put his mask back on.

When I took mine off, I understood why he'd replaced his.

Geronimo sniffed at my leg and growled.

I went to the shower and scrubbed all the way from my toes up to my knee just in case the jungle rot had spread beyond the confines of the cast. Then I doused the area with mouthwash.

Well, what did you expect? I didn't have any ankle wash.

I returned to the kitchen and said, "That was gross. You want some breakfast?"

He laughed. "Yeah, something aromatic to freshen the air."

I whipped up a pan of my desayuno de arroz, a combination of Chinese fried rice and standard Mexican rice. I fried four strips of bacon until they were extra crispy then threw in diced yellow onion and garlic and stirred them until softened, breaking the crispy bacon into pieces in the process and being careful not to burn the garlic. I added leftover yellow rice that was already flavored with cumin and coriander. The last step was to crack in four eggs and scramble them all through the mixture.

I retrieved two chilled champagne flutes and an equally chilled bottle of Gruet Blanc de Noir from the fridge, poured two glasses and made a toast. "To being back on two feet."

Tristan is the grandson of my aunt Beatrice. I call him my nephew, but he's more like a son to me. He attends the University of New Mexico, where his two main activities are majoring in computer science and fending off girls who find his olive complexion, bedroom eyes and unkempt curly hair irresistible. They also love his calm manner and easy smile.

He doesn't fend off *all* the girls, just enough of them to leave time for studying and for helping his uncle Hubert with things like removing my casts and abetting my excavations when technology is required.

After breakfast, I placed my atlas on the table and pointed to a spot just southwest of Oscura Peak.

"I want to go there."

"That's the place you had me show you on Google Earth."

I had a good reason for wanting to see that particular site. King Philip II granted permission to Juan de Oñate to explore Nuevo México and convert the native peoples to Christianity. Oñate entered New Mexico in 1598 and followed the Rio Grande, keeping a diary as he and his men traveled.

One diary entry describes the place I had in mind. Oñate lacked the technology to specify modern-day coordinates, but he gave accurate descriptions. The place in question—he called it *la cueva del clan topo* (the cave of the mole clan)—is in the Oscura Mountains, and his enumeration of the peaks to each side of it was all I needed.

I combined his description with my knowledge of the sort of terrain the cliff dwellers selected for practical and spiritual reasons and located a spot on the topographical map that fit the bill.

I was hoping that the coincidence of me using a topo map, as they are called informally, and *topo* being the Spanish word for "mole" was an omen.

Tristan looked up from the map. "I hadn't realized the place is inside the missile range."

I nodded. "I've tried to think of ways to get in using human interaction. Maybe convincing a high-ranking official to issue me a visitor's pass or getting some sort of work that would get me in."

He laughed. "Like becoming a missile repairman?"

"Something more suited to my talents. Maybe they need an archaeologist to help them comply with the Archaeological Resources Protection Act by inventorying sites for artifacts before they blast them into a haze of subatomic particles."

"I don't think the Defense Department has to play by ARPA rules."

He was probably right, although I did relish the idea of using ARPA to violate ARPA. But even if they did need an archaeologist, they wouldn't choose me. I was kicked out of the University of New Mexico graduate program for selling ancient pots. That was before ARPA, so it was perfectly legal for me to sell them. The department head claimed it violated the ethical standards of the discipline. Given that he spent most of the summer dig trying to get into the tent of one of the coeds, I didn't consider him an expert on ethics.

I think what motivated him to expel me was professional embarrassment. The site he chose for the dig turned out to be a dry hole, while my entrepreneurial venture a mile or so away yielded three pots that I sold for $25,000.

Or maybe he wanted to eliminate the competition. I was interested in that same coed. Like Dr. Gerstner, I also never saw the inside of her tent.

"I'm looking for a technological solution."

Tristan thought about it briefly. "You need to stay below the radar but above the rugged terrain. There is one ideal way to do that—a jet pack."

"One of those things you strap to your back and then swoosh up into the air? You're talking to your uncle, not George Jetson."

Tristan knows I have acrophobia. Not to mention aichmophobia, antlophobia and a number of others. If it has a Greek prefix, I probably have it.

"I could hike in at night with a flashlight, but a light could easily be spotted."

"They wouldn't need a light to spot you. They would know the instant you cross the perimeter."

"How?"

"They have a cool FiberPatrol FP2100-X perimeter intrusion detection system."

"And in English?"

"It's buried motion-sensing optic fiber. The moment you cross the cable, they know you're there."

"What if I jumped over it?"

"You can't jump over it because you don't know where it is. That's one of the beauties of the system."

I was beginning to wish he would concentrate more on defeating the system and less on praising it.

"I see utility-company workers walking around with hand-held devices that locate where their cables are buried and sticking little flags in the ground. Could you build me something like one of those that would detect where the perimeter-wire thing is so I'd know where to jump?"

He shook his head. "Because it's optic fiber, it's nonmetallic, produces no electric current and gives off no heat. So you can't locate it by detecting its magnetic field, electric energy or even by using infrared."

"Terrific. So how do they find it if a mole chews it in two and they need to repair it?"

"It sends them a signal telling them the GPS coordinates of the break."

I raised my hands in the surrender gesture.

5

After Tristan left, I gazed longingly at the bottle of Gruet from which only two glasses had been poured.

Much of New Mexico's charm derives from its rugged environs and equally rugged people. Gruet adds an unlikely touch of elegance, a bubbly from grapes grown near Truth or Consequences, bottled in Albuquerque and exported to four-star restaurants like the 21 Club in New York, where the wine list boasts Krug Clos du Mesnil ($1,875), Louis Roederer Cristal ($1,375) and of course Gruet ($57).

Sounds like a bargain unless you know that I can get it in Albuquerque for twelve bucks.

Madame Lilly Bollinger captured my attitude about champagne when she said, "I drink it when I'm happy and when I'm sad. Sometimes I drink it when I'm alone. When I have company, I consider it obligatory. I trifle with it if I'm not hungry and drink it when I am. Otherwise I never touch it—unless I'm thirsty."

I summoned up my meager willpower and stuck the Gruet back in the fridge. I had a date with Sharice that evening—my first sans cast—and wanted to be at my best in case . . . well, you know.

I opened the mail I had avoided for fear of what it contained. The mortgage notice was followed by a second notice for a hundred bucks from the doctor who spent five minutes with me to tell me it was okay to remove the latest cast. He offered to have his nurse do it, but I figured that was probably another hundred plus a fee for disposal of hazardous medical waste.

The mortgage was overdue, the electricity bill was overdue, the bill from the doctor was overdue, my MasterCard bill was overdue. The only bill not overdue was for my health insurance.

That's because I don't have any. Never have. Based on the figure the federal government claims is the average monthly cost of health coverage for someone like me who is self-employed, I've saved about $200,000 since opening Spirits in Clay.

I know, I know. One serious illness could wipe out that savings. It's a risk I'm willing to take. And one I will now be fined for taking. I don't mind paying the fine. It's a lot cheaper than buying insurance, and maybe the money I pay in will help someone.

I'm happy for people who benefit from the new law. I just don't want to spend money for something I hope never to use. It would be like owning a gun to protect my business. I'd rather take the risk than own the gun.

Perhaps this explains why I quit the first job I ever had in order to pursue an interest in pottery. Who wants an accountant who doesn't believe in protecting against risks?

The next bill I opened was also from a doctor, a nephrologist who treats Consuela Sánchez, the housekeeper, cook and nanny with whom I spent most of the first eighteen years of my life. The accumulated charges for various procedures I couldn't pronounce—much less understand—totaled $13,000, making my ankle doc seem like the Walmart of medicine.

Nephrologist sounds like someone who studies Queen Nefertiti of ancient Egypt. I guess if he called himself a kidney doctor, he couldn't charge such high fees.

Fortunately for the Sánchezes, they do have health insurance.

Unfortunately for me, I am that insurance. Knowing they would not accept money from me, I told them after my parents died that their estate provided health insurance for them. I don't feel comfortable with that lie, no matter how white it may be, but life is seldom perfect. I thought about trying to get them covered under the new law, but I couldn't figure out how to do that without them figuring out that I had been footing the bills all these years.

Which was never a problem for me until Consuela's kidney problems led to a transplant, which depleted my savings. I hadn't realized that the after-surgery care would continue to be so expensive.

One good Tompiro pot would banish my money woes.

Carl had a buyer. I didn't have the pot, but I had a hunch where I could find one.

I opened the shop and spent the day answering questions from a steady stream of customers, all of whom enjoyed their tour of the merchandise.

But not enough to actually buy any of it. Maybe I would make more money if I converted Spirits in Clay from a pottery shop to a pottery museum and charged an admission fee.

I closed at five and took Geronimo for a walk. Although he usually walks on my right, he insisted on staying to my left, away from the aromatic ankle, his keen sense of smell reassuring me that he is indeed a dog. I sometimes wonder about that because he has the physique of an anteater with his long neck and swaying gate.

I took a long shower, giving the stinky ankle a vigorous scrubbing. Cleaning it didn't improve its appearance—puffy and unnaturally white.

I hadn't driven in months. My Bronco was stolen just hours before I sprained my ankle. In fact, it was during the wilderness trek imposed on me by the loss of the vehicle that I sustained that injury.

Geronimo was supposed to be guarding the Bronco. His being a poor guard dog didn't surprise me. What surprised me was that he didn't go along with the thief for the ride. I managed to recover the Bronco without his help, but I hadn't driven it because of the cast.

When I turned the ignition switch, the only sound I heard was the tune I was singing, Gershwin's "Bidin' My Time," because that's what I'd been doing.

The battery was dead. I sang another two lines:

> But I'm bidin' my time,
> That's the kinda guy I'm

Time and *I'm*. They don't rhyme 'em like that anymore.

A dead battery was almost a blessing now that I could walk. I exited the Bronco and headed to Sharice's downtown loft, buoyed by the mere fact that I could do so on my own two feet. At the roundabout the city installed on Central—evidently thinking it makes Albuquerque a sort of United Kingdom with adobe—I sat down to rest.

After not being able to walk for months, I was out of shape.

A homeless woman emerged from Robinson Park and asked if I had any spare change so she could get something to eat. I pulled a handful of change from my pocket and gave her the four quarters it contained.

"If I had five dollars, I could get a full meal."

I don't consider five dollars to be *change*, but she evidently needed it more than I did, so I fished a five out with my left hand and held out my empty right one.

"Give me my quarters back."

She eyed my empty hand suspiciously. "Why?"

"So I can give you this five instead."

"How do I know you won't just take back the quarters and not give me the five?"

"Oh, for heaven's sake," I said and handed her the five.

"You don't really need these quarters, do you?" she asked once the fiver was safely in her possession.

"Yes, I do. I need them for bus fare."

She stared down at the change in her hand, evidently engaged in a moral debate.

In addition to the four quarters I gave her, I also had three dimes and a nickel, enough to pay the fare for Honored Citizens, the strange title the city has bestowed on the elderly, the young and the handicapped.

I once was young, I will be officially elderly in a little over a decade and I had been handicapped that very morning. There is no shame in these categories, but neither is there anything especially honorable about them. You don't *earn* them. They just happen to you.

The woman finally said, "I'll split it with you," and returned fifty cents to me.

Great. Now I was still fifteen cents short of full fare and had to use the Honored Citizens card even though I no longer had a cast.

6

~

I was tired and disillusioned by the time I finally punched Sharice's doorbell, but her radiance made it all better.

Her downtown condominium is urban chic—polished concrete floors, exposed metal beams, granite counters and enough stainless steel to build a shiny silo. You know you're in Albuquerque only if you look out the floor-to-ceiling windows toward the Sandia Mountains.

A black leather love seat, two Barcelona chairs, a glass coffee table and a matching glass dining table give a sparse look to the living room. I didn't know what the bedroom looked like because . . . well.

Her hard squeeze and wanton kiss made my spirits soar. Homelessness was ended in America. Everyone had a warm bed and food. All people were Honored Citizens. Buses were free for the handicapped, the uncapped and the capped.

She stepped back and twirled around to show me her back. All of it. Like every other dress in her designer collection, this one came demurely up to her neck in front. But unlike some of the others, it plunged to her waist in the back. It was made from what looked like aluminum filigree.

"It's from Alyce," she said, as if I knew the seamstress.

"I'm not falling for that again. I thought Vera Wang was an immigrant who worked in the back of a local Chinese laundry, but now that I know your passion for designer dresses, I'm guessing Alyce is from New York."

"Close," she said. "Paris."

I was in no mood to quibble, so I let slide the 3,600 miles between New York and Paris and handed her a stalk of yucca blossoms, elected by New Mexico schoolchildren in 1927 as the State flower, and known around here as *las velas de la Virgen*—the candles of the Virgin.

She took me by the hand. "I want to show you something."

She led me to the kitchen, opened the fridge and pointed to a bottle of Gruet Blanc de Noir.

"We'll have this with dessert."

"Which is?"

She flashed a devastating smile. "That depends on how the evening goes. Are you up for a night on the town?"

"Sure. I said I wanted to show you off as soon as I got rid of the cast."

She took my hands in hers. "That's sweet, Hubie. But remember what I told you. Some people will be unhappy to see us together."

"And remember what I told you, some people are—"

"I know—so unhappy about immigration issues that they won't like you dating a Canadian. I love that you take the high road, but you can't ignore the fact that I'm black and you're white."

"Actually, you're a fascinating shade of sepia and I'm a boring beige."

She handed me her jacket. "I'm taking you to Blackbird Buvette."

I'd walked by the place but never gone in because the customers look like characters in a B-grade film. On top of that, I didn't know what a buvette was. What would I say when an employee asked if she could help me? I'd like a massage? A puff on a hookah? A size-7 pith helmet?

Turns out it's a French word for a bar. I guess Sharice chose the place because she's from Montreal. It also has that edgy modern look she favors. Like her apartment, which she describes as form following function, whatever that means.

She clung to my arm during the walk. Most people just ignored the mixed couple. A few smiled at us. Albuquerque is generally a tolerant place. I wasn't worried about anyone making a scene.

But that's exactly what happened as I was taking the first bite of my green chile stew. A black guy wearing a black T-shirt over black jeans sauntered up to our table, looked at Sharice, flicked his thumb in my direction and said, "You can do better than him, sister."

I thought he was probably right, but I hoped she didn't.

Sharice replied, "*T'as une tête à faire sauter les plaques d'égouts.*"

The guy turned to me as if I were suddenly his ally and said, "Huh?"

"She doesn't speak English," I said. It seemed like the thing to say.

"Who are you?"

"Her translator."

"Yeah? Ask her if she'd like an English lesson. I speak it good."

I looked at Sharice and said, "*En croûte flambée crème anglaise.*"

She burst into laughter and said, "*Je préfère manger un torchon.*"

"What did she say?"

"I can't tell you."

He put his palms on the table and leaned into me with a mean smile. "Sure you can."

In fact, I couldn't. I don't speak French.

He bent in even closer as if performing push-ups on the tabletop, his biceps bulging as he lowered himself. The guy tending bar came out from behind it and was assessing the situation.

"She said you look like a hockey player."

"What's that supposed to mean?"

"I have no idea. I'm just the translator. French-Canadians have an odd sense of humor."

He stared at us for a moment. "Her loss," he said, and walked away. The bartender returned to his post.

"That was quick thinking, answering him in French. What was that first thing you said?"

"I said he has a face that could blow off a manhole cover."

I laughed, and she told me it's a common French-Canadian insult. Then she asked if I knew what I'd said.

"Sure. I said, 'In crust flamed English cream.'"

"Yeah, but why?"

"I had to say something. So I strung together some French words."

"And you threw in *anglaise* because you thought he might recognize the French word for *English*?"

"It was the best I could do at the spur of the moment."

"But why those particular words?"

"I learned them when I worked in a restaurant."

"You worked in a French restaurant?"

"No, an Austrian one called Schnitzel. But they still used French words. What was that second thing you said?"

"I said I'd rather eat a dishrag."

"Another French-Canadian insult?"

She nodded. "Here's another one you should learn: *nègre.*"

"Does that mean what I think it means?"

"It does."

"You hear that much?"

"Occasionally. Usually when the speaker doesn't know I'm a francophone."

She ate a bit of her green apple and walnut salad.

I spooned my stew. It was lukewarm.

"You okay?" she asked.

"Sure." I smiled at her. "I won't mind if you say you told me so."

"You said we shouldn't even acknowledge it."

"That's easy for me to say. No one has ever called me a *blanc.*"

She giggled. "How do you know that word? Wait, let me guess—*buerre blanc.*"

"I learned a lot of French words as a garçon."

"A garçon? I assumed you were the chef. I love your cooking."

"Thanks. I was at Schnitzel just to make plates, but I got pressed into service."

When I finally asked the waitress for our check, she said, "It's on the house. Sorry about that incident."

"It wasn't the restaurant's fault."

"We want everyone to enjoy this place. We don't think they should pay if they don't. Doesn't matter what the reason is."

I left her a big tip.

7

When she told me the dessert was beavertails, I figured it was more of that strange French-Canadian sense of humor.

Turns out it's a common Canadian dessert. No beavers are harmed during the preparation of the dish.

It's basically a buñuelo—fried dough sprinkled with sugar and cinnamon. The Canadian version gets its name from the shape of the pastry. Sharice's was fancier than its New Mexican cousin because she drizzled it with maple syrup and melted butter after it came out of the frying oil.

It was a good thing the Gruet was cold and dry.

We chatted about the beavertails and the champagne. We made small talk. No further mention was made of the incident at the café. She seemed nervous. I probably wasn't my happy-go-lucky self either, because I was struggling with whether to discuss what happened or just let it pass.

I decided the best course of action was to go home. "Thanks for the beavertails and the Gruet. What a great combo. It's late and—"

She was shaking her head. "I don't want you to go."

Normally, those words would have revved my pulse, but her face was filled with anxiety.

"Remember that day I gave you a black toothbrush to keep at your place for me just in case?"

"You want me to run home and bring it back? Even better, you want me to run home and bring *mine* back?"

She giggled. "I said there was something I needed to tell you."

"You're going to tell me now?"

Her anxious look reappeared. "No. I'm going to show you."

She took my hand and led me into her bedroom. Forget the anxiety on her face—my pulse was racing.

"Stand here."

She slid the dimmer switch to low then positioned herself so that the bed was between us. She turned her back to me. She unhooked a catch behind her neck. The dress fell to the floor. I already knew she wasn't wearing a bra, since Alyce of Paris had forgotten to sew a back on the dress and there was no place for any strap to hide.

The sight of Sharice naked save for white drawstring panties made it difficult to stay where she had put me, but I didn't want to spoil whatever she had in mind.

Her shoulders rose and fell from several deep breaths. Then she turned to me and I understood why her designer dresses reveal so much of her limbs and back and so little of her chest. Her petite right breast was perfect.

The scar where the left one had been was surprisingly small. She was shaking.

"Wow. You took your dress off. Does this mean we're finally going to have sex?"

"I'm showing you my scar, Hubie. It's awful."

"You think that's awful? That's nothing. Let me show you something really gross."

I took off my pants and hoisted my right leg onto the bed. "Look at that ankle. Did you ever see anything so disgusting in your whole life? It looks like I got a transplant from a mannequin. It's like something you might see immersed in a vat of formaldehyde in a biology lab. It looks like a slab of pork fat before it's fried into chicharrones."

It just came to me. Don't ask why, because I don't know. Having a tendency to react differently from most people is bad enough. But pair that with the lack of enough sense to keep those bizarre reactions to myself, and I frequently face Embarrassing Moments.

I clasped my hands together under my knee and swung my leg off the bed as if it were an inanimate object.

Then I looked up to see Sharice crying and thought, What an idiot I am. She's just done something incredibly difficult and courageous, and I'm acting the clown.

But she wasn't crying. Well, maybe a little. But mostly she was laughing. And she came around the bed and put her arms around me. We stayed in that embrace for several minutes. I didn't speak, because I was relieved that she hadn't been offended by my reaction, and I didn't want to press my luck.

"Will you stay with me tonight? I don't want to have sex. I just want you to hold me."

I pushed her away and smiled at her. "Is this a test of my willpower?"

"No. When it comes to me, I hope you have no willpower at all. It's just that I have a lot of things to deal with, and I have to do it one at a time."

"So should I go home and get those toothbrushes?"

"I'm a dental hygienist, silly. I have a whole box full of new ones."

Even though Sharice has seen more of the inside of my mouth than I have, it felt strange to be brushing, flossing and gargling with her. At least she didn't have that blue lab coat on. In fact, the only thing either of us had on at that point was underpants.

She took hers off before sliding under the covers. I took that as an invitation to follow suit.

After a long kiss, she said good night and rolled over onto her right side, a good move on her part because her wish that I have no willpower was coming true.

My right arm was under her neck, my right hand clasping hers. She found my left hand and placed it over her scar. I embraced her from behind, gently massaging the scar, hoping to palpate away any bad memories that might remain in her warm, lithe body.

We tossed and turned a bit but continued to snuggle because the windows were open and it was freezing cold.

At one point during the night, she felt my hands on her chest again and said, "It doesn't bother you?"

"No. I always sleep with the windows open."

She gave me a playful jab. "You know what I mean."

"The first time I saw you in Dr. Batres's office, you were so striking that I tried to picture you without any clothes on."

"Men."

"Yeah, we're all animals. When you dropped your dress tonight, the reality was a lot better than my imagination."

"Except in your imagination, you probably pictured me with two breasts."

"Neither of which was as cute as the one I'm touching now."

"But the left—"

"This is just a wild guess, but I'm going to say it was just like the right one. So reality is still better than imagination."

She kissed me, then turned and nodded off. After I lifted the covers on my side to let in some much-needed cold air, I finally did the same.

8

When I awoke the next morning, she was propped on her pillow smiling at me. "You're a sound sleeper."

I stretched while acknowledging as much. "How did you sleep?"

"Pretty good, considering your pesky little friend kept poking at me."

I felt my face glow red. "Sorry. I tried to think pure thoughts. I guess you have to go to work now."

"No. This is one of my ten-to-seven days. I planned a special breakfast for us."

"So you knew all along I'd be spending the night?"

"I was hoping you wouldn't turn me down."

She called the breakfast salmon Benedict. It was smoked salmon topped with a poached egg over a toasted English muffin slathered in béarnaise sauce dotted with capers, about as far from my traditional *desayuno* of huevos rancheros as Montreal is from Albuquerque. But it went just as well with the leftover Gruet.

After breakfast, she roasted green coffee beans. I was surprised it took only five minutes in her special roaster. The aroma was so good that grinding and brewing seemed almost superfluous.

Until she foamed some milk and gave me the best cappuccino I've ever tasted. I've never been a fan of fancy coffees, but I knew I could get hooked on Sharice's cappuccino.

She sat her empty cup down and said, "I'm going to tell you about my mastectomy."

"This is one of those things you need to do one at a time?"

"Yes. The second one. It will be a lot easier than the first one. After I tell you, we are never to speak of it again."

I nodded.

She looked me in the eyes. "The worst part wasn't the cancer. The worst part wasn't losing a breast. The worst part was the treatment. Everyone has side effects from chemotherapy. A lucky few have mild reactions. For most people, it's agony. For a small number of us, it goes beyond agony. I had a severe reaction to a drug called docetaxel. It sent me to the ER and then to the ICU for a week. It was so bad that I was disappointed I survived. They tried a lower dose the second time, but the result was just as bad. In addition to diarrhea, vomiting, trouble breathing, and throat swelling, my lips and mouth were so covered with sores that it was too painful to brush my teeth."

Her stare softened into a grin. "That was the worst part."

While we drank a second cappuccino, she told me about the rest of her grueling ordeal and how her bout with breast cancer brought her to Albuquerque.

She left for work. I volunteered to stay and do the dishes. Then I walked home singing "Fly Me to the Moon."

9

~

The first person through my door looked like the black version of that Mr. Clean guy pictured on the label of my kitchen cleaner. Except he didn't have an earring and was wearing a suit so perfectly tailored that you couldn't see the pistol holstered under the lapel.

It was Charles Webbe, the FBI agent who saved my life when the owner of the Austrian restaurant I worked in tried to murder me. I don't understand why the owner tried to kill me; all he had to do was wait for the food to do that.

"Heard you were involved in a racial incident," Charles said.

"The FBI is keeping tabs on me?"

"You think the CIA are the only ones who spy on ordinary citizens?" He laughed and then said, "The bartender at Blackbird Buvette is a friend. He told me James Mintars was hassling you and Miss Clarke."

"Is Mintars a big black guy?"

"Yes. And well known to the local police."

"So why should the FBI be involved?"

"The Bureau isn't involved. But if you want me to, I can have an informal talk with him." He smiled and added, "Brother to brother—make sure he doesn't bother you again."

Despite having a waistline no larger than mine, Agent Webbe is six-three and 225 pounds of muscle. A talk with him would put even Vladimir Putin on the straight and narrow.

"Thanks for the offer, but I don't think you need to do that. Sharice put him in his place—told him he had a face that could blow the cover off a manhole."

"*Une tête à faire sauter les plaques d'égouts,*" he said.

"You speak French?"

He nodded. "Russian too."

Maybe sending him for a talk with Putin was a better idea than I'd realized.

I brewed some New Mexico Piñon Coffee while we talked. I save the good stuff for people like Charles, who appreciate it.

When I handed him a cup, he commented on my remembering that he takes it without cream or sugar.

"How could I forget? When I first asked you how you took your coffee, you said, 'Black—like your girlfriend.'"

"I was just hassling you because you lied to me about having a black girlfriend."

"I *do* have a black girlfriend."

"You do now. You didn't then. Got any of those cuernos de azucar you fed me the last time I was here?"

"No, but I have some fresh buñuelos."

Buñuelos fly apart like clay pigeons when you bite into them, but Charles ate two without a single speck of the crisp fried dough showing on his dark-blue suit or starched white shirt.

The motto of the FBI is "Fidelity, Bravery, Integrity." Maybe they should add *Neatness*.

"I'm happy you're not worried about Mintars," he said, "but

there will be others. This is what happens when a white guy has a black girlfriend."

"I don't think of Sharice as black."

"You got a vision problem?"

"What I mean is I don't think of her as my 'black girlfriend.' That sounds like a phrase to distinguish her from my white one or my brown one. I have only one girlfriend. She just happens to be black. Just like I don't think of you as a black FBI agent. You're an agent who happens to be black. And I don't think of myself as a white treasure hunter. I'm a treasure hunter who happens to be white."

"You're not a treasure hunter of any color. You're a pot thief."

"You going to arrest me for that?" I asked with a smile.

"I'll leave that to the BLM." He put his empty cup on the counter. "Thanks for the coffee. I liked it."

He turned back after opening the door. "Your idealism is sappy, but I like it too."

After Charles left, my optimistic side hoped for a customer. My realistic side didn't share that hope, so I hung up my BACK IN FIFTEEN MINUTES sign and walked to Treasure House Books and Gifts on the south side of the Plaza. I counted five O'Keeffe posters along the way, as well as maybe a dozen of her flowers and bleached skulls adorning everything from calendars to T-shirts.

I suppose it was one of those cases of noticing things already on your mind, in this case the worn canvas Susannah thought was an O'Keeffe.

I bought three books, one by her, one about her and one with pictures of her New Mexico paintings.

Looking at those paintings made me think O'Keeffe liked New Mexico for the same reasons I do, but Susanna tells me you can't tell much about artists by looking at their work. For all we know, Andy Warhol never sipped a single spoon of Campbell's soup.

I wondered if she'd ever been in Old Town. Maybe even in my building before I owned it.

I wondered if she thought of Alfred Stieglitz as her Jewish husband or Juan Hamilton as her Hispanic boyfriend.

10

She gave me one of her looks. "*Consummate?* It sounds like a soup."

I had closed the shop with the inventory intact, alas, and had just told Susannah that although Sharice and I slept together, we didn't consummate our relationship. "It means—"

"I know what it means, Hubert. People don't use that word these days. What I don't understand is how you two slept together in the nude and didn't have sex."

"I thought pure thoughts."

"Right. Given what she said about your 'pesky little friend,' he evidently didn't get the no-sex-tonight memo."

Susannah loves pushing me over my embarrassment threshold, an easy task considering it's no higher than the salt rim on my margarita. Actually, the salt was gone and so was the margarita. I managed to run out of both simultaneously. No mean feat, considering I'd been talking about my date with Sharice rather than gauging the diminution of my drink.

She saw I had finished and signaled Angie for a second round. "Just last week we were trying to figure out her deep dark secret, although you weren't much help."

"At least I came up with three theories. You're the one who insisted we talk about it, and you didn't contribute anything."

"Your three theories were that she's a virgin, she's from Canada and she's thinking about becoming a nun. Compared to that, my nothing looks good. We should have kept at it. I think I would have figured it out."

"You would have guessed she had a mastectomy?"

She gave a little shudder. "Maybe not that specifically. But if a girl is hesitant about having sex even with a guy she really likes, one reason might be that she has a problem with her body."

"Like what?"

"I don't know. A hairy back? A tattoo of a walrus on her tummy? The point is it wasn't the sex *per se*—it was the getting naked part."

"That was my favorite part."

"Of course it was. You've been dying to see her in the altogether." She was silent for a moment. "It doesn't bother you at all?"

"How could getting undressed with Sharice bother me? Well, it bothered me in the sense that we didn't—"

"Yeah. Pesky. What I mean is doesn't it bother you that she . . ."

She didn't know how to finish that sentence and neither did I. If there's a politically correct way of saying *she no longer has a left breast* that makes you feel less uncomfortable, I don't know what it is.

"No, it doesn't bother me. I was so surprised at how small the scar was that I didn't think about what had been there." I hesitated. "I'm tempted to say something, but it might be oinky."

"That's never stopped you in the past."

"Okay, I'll just say it. I already knew she was flat-chested. I thought it went well with her thin, long limbs and petite features. You had a word for that look, but I don't remember it."

"*Gamine.*"

"Jeez, another francophone."

"That's like a bassoon, right?"

Sometimes I don't know if she's kidding. "So because she had small breasts to begin with, the operation didn't leave her looking lopsided."

She stared at me for a few moments. "I'm not sure if that's oinky or not."

"Whew. Anyway, I'm glad she showed me instead of telling me."

"Well, of course you are. You got to see her naked."

"Which was great, but that's not my point. My point is that if she'd *told* me, my imagination would have conjured up some horrible purply, bumpy disfiguration. But seeing it with no warning meant I hadn't mentally prepared for it. When she turned around, I just saw a scar. Actually, I just glanced at it. There was a lot of new and exciting scenery, so I didn't let my eyes stay in one place too long."

"Do you think that's why she didn't have reconstructive surgery?"

"No. She didn't have reconstructive surgery because she couldn't afford it."

"But she's from Canada. Isn't health care free up there?"

"My econ professor always reminded us there is no free lunch."

"Yeah, I know. It isn't free because they pay taxes for it. But pooling money together to cover health care makes sense."

"It does. But wouldn't it be better if it was pooled voluntarily rather than taxing Canadians who might want to spend their money on something else?"

"Like what?"

"I don't know. Hockey sticks and mukluks? Did I mention that Sharice roasts and grinds beans every time she makes coffee?"

"Twice."

"I guess I was impressed. Anyway, she told me the whole story while we were drinking the world's best cappuccino. She was in dental school when she found the lump. She suffered extreme side effects from the drug they gave her. The good news is she's been cancer-free for years. When the treatments ended, she wanted to consider reconstructive surgery, but there are very few cosmetic surgeons in Canada."

"Reconstructive breast surgery is not *cosmetic*, Hubert. It's not a facelift. For lots of women who've had a mastectomy, it reduces depression and raises self-esteem." She took a sip of her saltless margarita. "Jeez, I sound like a brochure from the Susan Komen Foundation."

I have no opinion on reconstructive breast surgery. Which is probably a good thing, because I don't think I have a right to an opinion on the subject.

"Reconstructive breast surgery may not be *cosmetic*," I pointed out, "but it's performed by cosmetic surgeons, and there are very few of them up there because the goal of the Canadian socialized medicine program is to keep people healthy, not make them look good."

She sighed. "I don't think they call it socialized medicine anymore."

"Whatever it's called, it doesn't cover facelifts and tummy

tucks, so that discourages doctors from pursuing the cosmetic surgery specialty. The result is that she faced a wait maybe as long as five years. She decided to do what many other Canadian women do—come to the US and pay for it. But she didn't have the money. So she decided to enter dental hygiene training because it takes a lot less time and money than going back to dental school. Her plan was to move to the States and make enough money as a dental hygienist to pay for a special operation that takes flesh from her butt and uses it to create a new breast."

"Sheesh. It's not called *taking flesh from her butt and using it to create a new breast*. It's called autonomous breast reconstruction."

"And you know about this because?"

"I volunteered at the Walk for the Cure and filled the time between registering walkers by reading brochures. It was interesting in a sort of morbid way."

"Well, it's not *autonomous*—it's *autological*. I remember because Sharice loves word games."

"Autological is a game like Scrabble?"

"I don't know if there's a commercial board game, but the way Sharice taught me is one person names a letter and the other person has to think of an autological word starting with that letter. Then you switch, and the first person to be stumped loses."

"What's an autological word?"

"One that describes itself. Like *noun* or *short*."

"Because *noun* is a noun and *short* is a short word?"

"Exactly. Want to try a round?"

"Sure. I'll start," she said with her usual enthusiasm. "Give me one starting with *a*."

"Avoidable."

"How is that autological?"

"Because the word itself can be avoided."

"Oh, right. Give me a letter."

"*O.*"

I thought about it while she did and couldn't think of one. I was wishing I'd given her an easier letter when she said, "Old."

"That's good. I couldn't think of one that starts with *o.*"

"Here's another one—*olde.*"

"You already said that."

She shook her head. "This one has an *e* on the end."

"Wow. You're as good at this as Sharice is. She always beats me."

Angie arrived with our second round. I sipped my New Mexican limeade—also known as a margarita—to make sure it was as good as the last one. It was.

Susannah asked me why Sharice hadn't yet had the reconstructive surgery.

"Dental hygienists don't make all that much, and the operation is really expensive, so I—"

"No! Please tell me you didn't volunteer to help her pay for it."

"Of course not. Volunteering to pay would make it sound like it matters to me."

"That is so understanding."

"And on top of that, I like the way her butt looks and don't want a scar on it."

She threw a chip at me.

"Charles Webbe came to see me today."

"They're probably still trying to figure out where all the money from Schnitzel went."

"I don't doubt it, but that wasn't why Charles dropped in." I told her about the incident at Blackbird Buvette. "Charles offered to have a man-to-man talk with the guy who hassled Sharice. He also predicted more problems, said that's what happens when a white guy has a black girlfriend."

"And you probably told him about one of your SAPs."

I have a growing list of astute observations about humankind. Each is a Schuze Anthropological Premise, abbreviated by Susannah as SAP because she says that's what you have to be to believe them.

"No, but I did tell him I don't think of Sharice as my black girlfriend. I think of her as my girlfriend who happens to be black."

"I know you think that's a significant distinction, but most people probably think it's splitting hairs."

"Before you were dating Baltazar, you dated Rafael Pacheco. Do you think of those two as your Hispanic boyfriends?"

"No. I think of Baltazar as a nice guy with sexy eyes. And since Rafael slithered away, I think of him as a snake."

I laughed. "I wonder if Georgia O'Keeffe thought of Juan Hamilton as her Hispanic boyfriend."

"Juan Hamilton isn't Hispanic. His real name is John Hamilton. His parents were missionaries or something in Latin America, and he grew up there and adopted the name Juan. And the rumors about him being her boyfriend may or may not be true. He was fifty years younger than her, but I'd like to think they were lovers just to turn the tables on that geezer Stieglitz."

"But she and Stieglitz were at least married."

"Right. He was fifty-eight when they met and the most powerful person in the entire art world. She was twenty-eight years old and totally unknown."

"Maybe it was true love."

"More like true lust. He used her, Hubie. He used the apartment he lived in with his wife to take nude photographs of O'Keeffe and deliberately timed it so that his wife would walk in on them. She threw him out, which is what he wanted but didn't have the courage to ask for."

"Well, he *did* make her famous."

"He made her famous initially, but she made him famous in the long run. He wouldn't be as widely known today if it weren't for her. And someone else would have eventually shown her work. It was the paintings that made her famous, not the man."

I thought about the nudes of O'Keeffe we saw in the exhibit Susannah took me to. There was something creepy about knowing her husband took those photos.

In addition to the early nudes, there are thousands of other pictures of O'Keeffe, some of the most famous taken when she was in her eighties, her fierce independence more obvious than in the younger years. The wrinkles from the New Mexico sun couldn't hide her beauty, even in her eighties and nineties. No wonder there were rumors about her and Hamilton. She was the most photographed woman of the twentieth century. I thought about the words to Elton John's "Candle in the Wind":

> *Your candle burned out long ago*
> *Your legend never did*

I doubt that Georgia O'Keeffe worried about her legend. She was too busy doing what she loved.

11

⌒

Susannah left for her night class—it's Modern American Painters this semester—and I strolled back across the plaza knowing my cupboard was bare. I hadn't bought groceries in weeks because getting to the store by bus and returning with sacks while using crutches was too much hassle. And now that the cast was off, the battery in the Bronco was dead.

It's hard to save either money or your waistline living on restaurant food. I was craving something simple. What I got instead was spaghetti pie, courtesy of Miss Gladys Claiborne, proprietor of the eponymous Miss Gladys's Gift Shop two doors down from me, where she took up residence after her husband died. Most owners of the galleries, eateries and specialty stores in Old Town retreat to their suburban homes after locking up for the day. Miss Gladys and I are the only two on our street who actually live here, and we have a symbiotic relationship. I provide security for her, and she provides food for me.

The reality falls short of the theory.

As a woman raised in a bygone age, she believes a man provides security. Fortunately, she has never needed me to come to her rescue. I suspect she would put up a better fight against an intruder than I would.

Her cooking . . . No, you can't call it that. *Assembling* is the more accurate word. Her casseroles are assembled from ready-to-eat foods used in the exact quantity of the packages they are sold in. Thus, teaspoons, tablespoons and cupfuls give way to cans, jars, bags and cartons.

Her spaghetti pie contains one package of spaghetti, one bag of Parmesan cheese, one can of Wolf Brand Chili, one can of Ro*Tel Original Diced Tomatoes & Green Chilies, one container of Philadelphia Savory Garlic cooking cream and one bag of shredded mozzarella cheese.

"The spaghetti and Parmesan make the crust. Doesn't that just beat all? You just throw them together and press them against the bottom and sides of a baking dish. Then you dump in the can of chili and the Ro*Tel. You mix the cream cheese and mozzarella together for the topping. Then just bake it until the crust is golden."

As usual, she brought the casserole in a bag made from gingham and embroidered with an image of the gazebo in the plaza. I don't know what gingham is made from, but it must be a sturdy fabric to hold a ceramic plate, a glass baking dish in a cozy warmer and a thermos of sweet tea.

The fact that she can carry such a load is the basis for my assessment of her odds against an intruder.

Although Miss Gladys's concoctions are seldom on the approved foods list of the American Heart Association, some of them are surprisingly tasty. This one was not. I know this is almost un-American, but I do not like pasta with its slimy texture and cardboard taste. The only reason people think they like it is because it's usually slathered with marinara or some other misuse of perfectly good tomatoes.

"Just look at that," she said, her blue eyes sparkling. "The spaghetti is the exact color of a pie crust and the mozzarella topping looks like buttercream frosting."

"Maybe I should save it for dessert."

She laughed at my ploy to avoid eating the pie and poured me some sweet tea. The fact that I was able to choke it down with a smile is testament to my fondness for Miss Gladys.

12

The indigestion started only minutes after Miss Gladys departed. I was beginning to think Wolf Brand Chili must be named after its main ingredient.

The Old Town Guild was having one of their dreaded Business After Hours events at La Placita. I walked to the southeast corner of the plaza and crossed the street into the eatery where Susannah works the lunch shift.

Despite the fact that I rarely attend these events, my name tag sat on a table next to those of the other no-shows. I pinned it to my jacket and headed for the hors d'oeuvres table, where I found the perfect remedy for spaghetti pie—pico de gallo, a proper use of the noble tomato. I spooned some onto a plate, grabbed some tortilla chips and stepped into the line for the cash bar.

A man fell in line behind me and said, "Hello. I'm Glad."

"About what?"

"No, that is my name, short for Gladwyn," he said, pointing to his name tag, which read Gladwyn Farthing.

"I'm Hubie," I said.

"Your name badge is wrong."

I looked down to see if I had picked up the wrong tag.

"No, that's my name—Hubert."

"I meant you have it in the wrong place. You should pin it on your right lapel."

"I'm left-handed."

"Doesn't matter, does it? You still shake with your right hand, which means you should have your tag on the right because that's the side people see as they shake your hand."

Now I remembered why I don't attend these things—inane conversations.

As you may have guessed from his name, he was English. He looked to be in his sixties. He sounded like a character in *Downton Abbey* but looked like one in Looney Tunes; namely, Porky Pig. Pursed lips, pink skin and a blunt nose.

"Thanks for the tip about name tags," I said, hoping thusly to bring our chat to an end.

"Doesn't matter you have it on incorrectly. I already knew who you are."

"Oh?"

"I'm told you may have commercial space to let."

I was waiting for him to finish the sentence when it dawned on me that he was using *let* the way we use *lease*.

"I do have a vacant space, but I don't have it listed."

"I didn't get the information from an estate agent. I got it by asking about. Have you any interest in letting it?"

Letting it what? I wondered.

My shop and residence are in an adobe built by Don Fernando María Aranjuez Aragon in 1683. At some point during its 333 years of existence, it was divided into three parcels. I own the east third. Miss Gladys owns the west third. I lease the middle third from Benny Orozco, who is descended from Don Pablo

Benedicion Verahuenza Orozco, who bought the building from its original owner for fifteen pesetas in 1691.

When the middle third became vacant, I leased it because I thought I wanted two shops, one featuring traditional Native American pottery and one featuring my copies. Running two stores proved to be a hassle, so I reconsolidated.

Now the leased space sits empty while I make monthly payments. It makes no economic sense, but at least I've come to realize why I leased it in the first place. It wasn't because I needed two shops. It was because I didn't want to risk having a body-piercing emporium or pawn shop as a neighbor.

"How would you use the space?" I asked Glad.

"Casual clothing—jumpers, trainers, plimsolls, swimming costumes—that sort of thing."

The perfect business, right? Nothing noisy or open late. No rowdy customers. No cooking smells. Never mind that I have no idea what a plimsoll is and that a bathing costume sounds like something Esther Williams would wear at Halloween. This could be a way to get those lease payments made by someone else.

"I might be interested. Would you like to see the space?"

"I have already done so. Looked through the glass door, you see."

No, I thought to myself, if you looked through the glass door, I wouldn't see—*you* would see.

"How much will you let it for?"

"It's a thousand square feet, and retail space in Old Town goes for about a dollar a foot."

"A thousand a month is beyond my budget. I have a proposal. The town I come from, Ludlow, is home to many sole-proprietor shops. When the shopkeeper has to run an errand or visit a doctor's surgery, he closes up and posts a notice. We in England are used to it. But you Yanks seem less patient. You expect shops to keep regular hours."

I could have sworn he said *shoppes*. I could almost hear the extra letters. I nodded my agreement to his observation.

"I propose that I mind your store when you are away, and in consideration thereof, you reduce the lease to eight hundred."

Since eight hundred is the exact amount I was paying Benny Orozco, I was tempted to accept his offer on the spot. But I hesitated.

"I'll stand you a drink," he said.

We had reached the front of the line. He ordered a pink gin. I asked for a Tecate. He paid. We found a table, worked out the details and made a toast to our new business arrangement. The good fortune of meeting Glad was a small step toward solvency.

13

~

Sharice walked into Spirits in Clay the next day around noon with a young cheetah on a leash.

Geronimo yelped, then bolted headlong into the door to the workshop. Bouncing off it didn't injure him—his head is more skull than brain. He popped back up and began clawing furiously at the door, looking back every few seconds to make sure the cheetah was still on its leash.

I took pity on him and opened the door.

"Sorry," she said, laughing. "I should have called to warn you, but I wanted it to be a surprise. I don't like laughing at Geronimo, but you have to admit he doesn't quite live up to his name."

I made a feeble attempt to defend his courage. "Well, he's never seen a cheetah before."

"It's not a cheetah. It's a Savannah cat."

"Wow. They grow them big in Georgia." The beast was twice the length of a dachshund and a whole lot taller—it came up past Sharice's knees.

"It's not from Georgia. Savannah cats are a cross between a serval and a domestic cat."

"I know cats are domestic, but I've never known one to be servile. Only dogs seem anxious to serve their masters."

"Not *servile*. *Serval*, with the accent on the first syllable. Servals are a breed of wild cats from Africa."

"Africa?"

"Don't worry, it's not an ethnic thing. I'm not going to start wearing dashikis and grand boubous." She laughed. "Unless they're designed by Coco Chanel or Yves Saint Laurent."

She let the animal off its leash, took a beanbag from her pocket and threw it in my direction. The cat sprung into the air and caught the beanbag in flight. Then he landed on the counter in front of me. He leaned in my direction and stared into my eyes. Then he gave me a swat on the nose, jumped off the counter and returned the beanbag to Sharice.

"He plays fetch?"

"He does." She threw the beanbag at the door. He ran it down, brought it back and dropped it at her feet.

"He likes you, Hubie."

"He took a swipe at me."

"Yeah, but he kept his claws in. That means he likes you."

Probably a good thing. It was clear I'd be unable to fend off an attack from him, and Geronimo had already demonstrated how much help he'd be.

"His name is Benz. Kathy bought him about a year ago, but she has to give him up because she's marrying a guy who's afraid of him."

"At least he has some sense, although marrying Kathy makes me wonder."

Kathy is one of the other assistants in Dr. Batres's office. She cleaned my teeth the first time I went there.

"I'd forgotten you know her. Why did you ask for a change?"

I couldn't hide the sheepish grin. "I saw you in the next room."

"I'm glad you switched."

"Me too."

"Servals tend to be like dogs—attached to one person. So before I agreed to take him, I had a long talk with Erik and Kurt Durnberg, the guys who sold him to Kathy. Funny you mentioned Georgia. The Durnbergs' cattery is right next-door in Florida. It has a cool name: Soignés Savannahs."

"More French. What does it mean?"

"Elegantly dressed."

"Describes you both."

"Thanks. Erik and Kurt told me Savannahs can also have an attachment to a second person, and for Benz, that's me. I would cat sit when Kathy was away. I fell in love with him the first time he stayed with me. I was still living in that dreary apartment on San Mateo, and he cheered me up. I wasn't dating, so he was about the only company I had away from work." She paused. "I'm hoping you'll be spending a lot of time at my place."

"Me too."

"You won't mind Benz being there?"

"Not at all. You two look stunning together—both so lean and lithe. But I may have to put Geronimo in therapy."

14

⁓

That cinches it. She's in love with you. And she sees it as permanent. Wait . . ." She cupped a hand to her ear. "Are those wedding bells I hear?"

"Just because she got a cat?"

"It's not getting the cat—it's the timing. She was living all alone in what she admits was a dreary apartment, and she loved having Benny for company."

"Benz," I corrected.

"With a *z* like in Mercedes?"

"Mercedes doesn't have a *z*."

"Sheesh. Anyway, the cat is the only bright spot in her life. But she doesn't buy one or adopt one from the shelter. And why not?"

She took a sip of her margarita and looked at me.

"She's allergic to cats?"

"Why would she take Benz if she's allergic to cats?"

"Because Savannah cats are hypoallergenic."

"Really?"

"That's what she told me."

"Well, that's not the answer. The reason she didn't get a cat was because she wasn't dating."

"That doesn't make sense. Not dating is all the more reason to have a pet for companionship."

"I figured you wouldn't understand. She wasn't dating, but she was *hoping* to. Believe me, I know. I've been there too many times. So she didn't get a cat for fear of becoming a cat lady."

"Cat Lady is one of those superheroes like Batman, right?"

"Wrong. A cat lady is an unmarried woman who dotes on her cat. In severe cases they can lose interest in dating because they're so wrapped up in the life of their cat. Or cats—usually they begin to collect them like stamps."

"Except you have to lick stamps, whereas cats take care of that themselves."

She just shook her head. "So now that she has a boyfriend, she doesn't have to worry about being a cat lady, so that's why she took Benz."

"No. She took Benz because Kathy had to give him up. It's just a coincidence that it happened while she and I are dating."

"Men are clueless."

I didn't dispute the point.

"Tell me about Glad."

"He ordered a pink gin."

"What's a pink gin?"

"Gin with a dash of bitters."

"Yuck. Probably need a stiff upper lip to drink it. Why is he called Glad?"

"It's short for Gladwyn."

"I'll bet he's Welsh, and his last name is full of *w*'s and *l*'s, something like Llewellyn. He probably comes from a town with a name like Caerfyrddin or Llanymddyfri."

She pronounced them "Carmarthen" and "Landovery," but how would I know if she got them right?

"He came from Ludlow, and his last name is Farthing."

"It's a good thing he didn't shorten that one to the first four letters."

"You really are clever with words."

"You have to be to know how to pronounce Caerfyrddin and Llanymddyfri."

"It probably helps that your last name is Inchaustigui. Is Welsh related to Basque?"

"Funny you should ask. The languages aren't related but the people are. The Basque were the first people to arrive in the British Isles after the last Ice Age. Over eighty percent of the Welsh today still have DNA from those early Basque settlers."

"One of my Schuze Anthropological Premises is that culture is not genetic. DNA has nothing to do with language."

"I don't need one of your SAPs to know that. The Basques in England were overrun by Celts and adopted their language. But maybe speaking Basque limbers up the tongue for weird Welsh words."

"At any rate, I don't think Glad is Welsh. He looks nothing like Tom Jones."

"He probably doesn't look like Catherine Zeta-Jones either."

"No. More like Porky Pig."

"I think having him mind your shop will increase your income."

"I doubt it. An Anasazi pot is not an impulse purchase. I figure if they really want one, they'll come back when I'm there."

"And if you're not there the second time, they might go somewhere else."

"There is no somewhere else. If they want genuine ancient pots, I'm almost the only game in town."

"But they might decide your shop being closed is the perfect excuse to buy that Porsche they've always wanted."

"People who appreciate ancient pottery have too much class to drive flashy cars."

"Let's make a wager. Track your total sales for the next month and compare it to last month. If sales are higher, it will be because Glad is keeping the shop open for normal business hours."

Susannah loves wagers. Gambling is chancy, and you already know how I feel about taking risks. But wagering with Susannah is fun because the stakes are always wacky. In the most recent wager, the agreement was that she had to keep her car if she lost, and I had to take it if I lost.

I said, "If he sells one pot, that would be higher than last month, so that's not a fair test."

"Okay, you figure out how to test it. I'll figure out what to bet. And we'll have a small test this Thursday. You'll be gone all day. We'll see if Glad makes a sale in your absence."

"I'm not going anywhere Thursday."

"You are. You just don't know it yet." She flashed that mischievous smile she does so well, only one side of her lips curled up and the opposite eyebrow raised. "Thursday is the day they let visitors go to the Trinity Site."

"We already talked about that. There is no way I could leave the road and drive to the Oscura Mountains without being spotted."

"I agree. That's why I'm going with you."

The mischievous smile gave way to the knowing grin.

"What's the plan?"

"I drive. At some point, I pull over and you jump out. You scurry into an arroyo and make your way to the ancient ruin. I continue on to Trinity Site. I hang around there all day, then pick you and your new pots up on the way out."

"Would that give me enough time?"

"If we enter when they open at eight, I can drop you off by eight fifteen at the latest. I'll have to pick you up by one forty-five to make it back to the gate by two when they close it. That gives you five and a half hours. Let's call it five because we don't want to cut it too close. It's four miles from the road to the place you showed me on the map. Your ankle seems to have regained most of its strength, so you should be able to cover that in less than three hours round-trip. That leaves you almost two hours to dig."

"Wow, you have it all planned out. But that's a lot of driving for you, and I might come up empty."

"Not knowing is half the fun."

"Okay. When do we leave?"

"Two a.m."

"Two a.m.?"

"A line forms at the gate long before they open. We need to be at the front of it."

15

Which is why we were cruising down Interstate 25 in total darkness Thursday morning.

If you're thinking this is when I encounter the black helicopter, you're jumping ahead too far.

Susannah had recharged the battery on my Bronco because she figured it was better suited to the rough White Sands roads than her old Crown Vic with its chronic oversteer.

It would be Glad's first day minding the shop. I'd given him a key the day before we left. I also left a note that read "Make coffee and sell pots. At the end of the day, turn off the coffee maker, empty the trash and wash the windows."

The last item was a joke. But if he didn't realize that, I'd have clean windows.

We left the interstate at San Antonio, famous as the birthplace of Conrad Hilton and the home of the Owl Bar and Café, whose green chili cheeseburgers are more popular with New Mexicans than any hotel chain can ever hope to be. Unfortunately, we passed through the sleepy village of 150 people at five in the morning, too early for a cheeseburger.

We were the first vehicle to arrive at the Stallion Gate on

the north side of the missile range on the day of the Trinity Site Open House. After we showed our driver's licenses and car registration to the MP at the gate, I took a nap in the backseat.

I'm not used to getting up at two in the morning.

Susannah woke me when the gate was opened, waved goodbye to the MP and pulled away at normal tourist speed. Around the first curve and out of sight of the gate, she switched from tourist to NASCAR driver, explaining that she wanted to put some distance between us and the cars behind so that she could let me out while we had the road to ourselves and no witnesses to my leaving the Bronco.

She skidded to a halt by a shallow draw. I jumped out at a dead run and was ten yards down the draw when she took off. I don't know how far I had gone when the car behind us at the gate passed by because I had followed the draw through a couple of turns and could no longer see the road.

More important, the road could no longer see me.

So far, so good.

I was dressed in brown hiking boots, khaki pants, a long-sleeve khaki shirt and a beige Tilley hat, an outfit that protected me both from the sun and—I hoped—from detection. The idea was to blend in to the desert terrain. My web belt held binoculars, a canvas canteen, a hunting knife, a compass and a piece of quarter-inch rebar.

I scanned the area with the binoculars. There were some structures on the hills off to my right. I hoped they contained radar rather than one guy drinking coffee and another asking, "Who's the short guy in the khaki outfit?"

The United States Geological Survey created over fifty thousand maps that show landform details of the entire country. If you do the math and divide the number of maps into the total area of the Unites States, you'll discover that each map covers a square area roughly seven miles on each side. An hour and a half after rolling out of the Bronco, I was standing under an outcrop of the Oscura Mountains studying USGS map number 193371.

The spot I wanted was close to a contour line that marked 6,800 feet of elevation. The road to the Trinity Site is just below 5,000 feet. So the four-mile hike had taken me up almost 2,000 feet.

I scoped the face of the outcrop. Tristan had shown me a satellite picture of it on Google Earth. Now I was seeing it from a much better perspective—that of *Mother* Earth. Most people would not have known what to look for. I did.

It was the sort of location the ancients built in. Finding the path up to it took half an hour. I was a bit behind schedule but feeling confident because the return hike would be downhill. Perfect for that gunnysack full of pots I imagined myself carrying.

I probed the soil in front of and inside the rooms for almost an hour and was rewarded with nothing more than rocks and animal bones.

I was about to give up. I sat down in one of the rooms and studied it. The walls were stone and mud, the roof formed by the natural overhang so that the room height sloped from six feet at the front to four feet at the back. The opening in the rear wall was too small even for me. I removed a portion of it and crawled into a triangular space. The air was cool and still. The soil was loose. I returned the rebar to my belt and dug out a perfect Tompiro pot with my hands.

And measured it with them. It was three hands tall and two wide.

I smoothed the dirt over the hole. I went to the ledge and

gathered some soil, less sandy and with more clay than the soil in the space behind the room and therefore more suited to making mortar. I mixed the soil with water from my canteen and replaced the stones I had dislodged, mortaring them to match the rest of the wall.

As the Park Service likes to say: "Take nothing but memories—Leave nothing but footprints."

I modified the saying a bit: "Take only pots—Don't leave even footprints."

I ran my hands over the smooth surface of the pot and closed my eyes. I saw a woman crush limonite and ochre in a metate. Saw her mix the powder with water and willow sap and combine the mixture with wet clay to form a pigmented slip. Saw a yucca leaf slit to the width of the line she wanted and dipped into the slurry. Watched the yucca go limp in the liquid. After chanting a prayer, she began painting the geometric pattern.

I opened my eyes and looked at her design, rectangles of varying sizes, some overlapping, each filled with hatching. Bold vertical stripes. Lines, nothing more. Monochromatic. But organic in a way Mondrian's paintings could never be.

Metaphysical.

There are those who would say what I did is reprehensible. I disturbed a holy place. Stole a pot. Prevented it from being studied in situ by professional archaeologists.

I don't care what those people think. I've made my peace with what I do. The woman who made that pot has been dead for four hundred years. I can't tell you her name, but I can show you who she was by bringing her creation back into history.

Because she couldn't read or write, the Spaniards labeled her uncivilized. But her ability to make and read petroglyphs is the same skill exercised in a different way. The markings on her pot had as much meaning for her as the words in a book do for us. The lines and angles didn't make her pots stronger or improve their capacity to store seeds. They are there because the potter was answering Whitman's question, "What good amid these, O me, O life?"

The powerful play does indeed go on, and she contributed a verse.

The Tompiro were a peaceful people, skilled masons who quarried stone and built beautiful multistory dwellings. Most of these were on the open plains to the north, close to the dry lake beds where the Tompiro gathered the salt they traded to nomadic tribes for animal skins. They used this place when the seasons changed or they wanted to hide from the Apache.

After two Spaniards were allegedly killed by some Tompiro, Juan de Oñate destroyed three of their pueblos, killing nine hundred men, women and children in the process.

During a winter when many Tompiro froze to death for lack of firewood, the Franciscan priests forced Tompiro slaves to make six hundred wooden crosses.

Less than a hundred years after the arrival of the Spaniards, the Tompiro ceased to exist. An entire people wiped off the face of the Earth. A million pots will not bring them back. But the one pot I recovered reminds us that they lived, and that one woman among them created a thing of beauty that can still stir the hearts of men.

There was probably more loot, but it was time to go. I pulled up a clump of grama grass and used it as a broom, sweeping the sand behind me until I hit the rocky part of the trail.

I placed the pot in the gunnysack and hung it on my back

with a rope. I didn't want the pot in my hands or in front of me if I fell. An unnecessary precaution, as it turned out. I didn't fall or even stumble. The downhill walk was as easy as I had hoped. Or maybe I just felt light on my feet because I'd found an ancient pot. Touched the past.

I neared the point where Susannah had dropped me off. She was standing on the shoulder of the road talking to an MP. His jeep was next to the Bronco.

I buried the pot behind a dune, sticking the rebar next to it with some of it protruding as a marker. I used my compass to note the degree readings of two peaks to the east and a small hill to the west. I dribbled a bit of water from the canteen onto my pants. I walked to the road.

To Susannah I said, "Thanks for stopping," and to the MP, "Good afternoon."

He looked so lean and hungry in his camouflage uniform that I fancied his name was Cassius. His military bearing and courtesy seemed forced.

"Good afternoon, sir. You are not supposed to leave the road."

"Sorry. I just couldn't hold it any longer."

He looked at my pants. "That's what Miss Inchaustigui was just telling me. May I see your ID, please?"

I handed him my driver's license. He checked it against a list and gave it back to me.

"You should have no trouble reaching the gate before two."

He stared at me as I climbed into the Bronco and was still staring when we rounded a corner and he slid out of the rearview mirror.

16

Well, you warned me you might come up empty."

We were bumping along toward Stallion Gate.

"I didn't come up empty. I found a perfect Tompiro pot. It's buried back there about fifty yards from where you were waiting for me."

"Why did you bury it?"

"I didn't want to. My first thought was to keep it in the gunnysack and hope the MP wouldn't ask about it. Then I remembered our cover story. If I left the road because I had to pee, why would I have taken along a gunnysack with a big pot in it?"

"Because you wanted a pot to pee in?"

I started to reply but realized she was joking.

"I see your point," she said. "He probably would have asked about it. He looked you over pretty good."

"Yeah, he was staring at the wet spot on my pants."

"Did you really have to embellish the act by dribbling water on your pants? It *was* water, right?"

I didn't dignify that with an answer. I asked instead if it was the same MP who was at the gate that morning. It had been dark and I was sleepy. I didn't get a look at him.

"No, he was at the site all day and shooed everyone out when it was time to leave. I was one of the last to go. I let people pass until there was no one behind me. I didn't want anyone to see me pick you up. What I didn't realize was that after everyone left, the MP at the site would come along behind us. He must have had to tidy up a bit because he was not in sight when I stopped to wait for you. So how do we retrieve our pot?"

"I have no idea."

"Maybe we just wait until the next time they open the Trinity Site."

I shook my head. "That's a year from now. I need the money now." I looked over at her. "Must be lonely being an MP inside the missile range. Maybe he'd let a pretty young lady sneak in to recover our pot."

"I must have left my feminine mystique at home. He didn't even tell me his name. What do you mean, *our* pot?"

"The wheelman shares in the loot."

"Excellent. What's the pot worth?"

"Wilkes offered thirty thousand for it."

"He offered you twenty-five for that Mogollon jug, and you never saw a penny of it."

"He says the buyer this time is more reliable—a big-time collector with deep pockets."

I told her about my mental video of the woman who made the pot.

"I know why you're not married. You're in love with the ancient potter women."

For all I know, she may be right. But I think the reason I'm not married is because all through high school and college I was the bookish type of kid girls weren't interested in. I never had a serious girlfriend until I was in my late twenties. By then I was running a pottery store and living behind the shop.

I've settled into the bachelor life. A living space that doesn't demand much upkeep, my own cooking, which I like, and a workshop for my potting. Women seem to like me more now, but I don't think it's because I've become less bookish, and I haven't become taller either. Or sculpted. My only six-pack has *Tecate* written on it.

The simple truth is I do better with the ladies now because they have fewer choices. Ask any single woman over thirty-five how often she meets a guy who's unattached, easy to get along with and has no bad habits.

Well, I drink a bit more than I should and I steal pots. But no one's perfect.

And now I have a nephew who's like a son, and companionship with Susannah.

All that's missing is the *S* word. I have the occasional fling with a woman, but haven't yet been flung as far as marriage. I thought about it with Dolly Aguirre, but that didn't work out.

As we headed back to Albuquerque, I was thinking about it with Sharice. I like her better than anyone I've dated before. Of course, at that point I was still wondering about that list of things she had to deal with one at a time, so maybe—

"How much is my share?"

I hadn't thought about it.

"What do you think is fair?" I asked her.

"Ten percent?"

"That's pretty low."

"All I did is drive."

"No. You hatched the plan. And you took the same risk I did.

If they discovered I didn't leave the road just to pee, they would charge both of us with trespassing. Or maybe even espionage."

"That's a stretch. Okay, here's the wager. If Glad increases sales, I get twenty percent. If not, I settle for ten."

17

Glad came in the next morning and handed me my key.

"Keep it," I said. "I have others, and you can let yourself in when I need you to be here."

"I'm happy to take a key each time I mind the shop, but I prefer to leave it on the counter and let the door lock behind me as I leave."

I understand that having a key to someone else's place can be discomfiting, so I just nodded my assent.

He then gave me something much better than a key—$800.

"You've already paid the first month in advance," I noted.

"The money is not from me. I sold that small white bowl with the many black lines."

"If you're going to mind the shop, you might as well learn the merchandise. We don't call those bowls. They're called *ollas*. And that line pattern is from the Acoma Pueblo."

His pink face reddened with enthusiasm. "Smashing. What are *ollas* used for?"

"The glazed ones are used for stews, the unglazed ones for water. But most of the ones made these days aren't used for anything. They've progressed—or perhaps regressed—from utensil to artwork. My friend Susannah said having you cover for me might increase sales, but I didn't expect it to happen on your first day on duty."

"I was a bit jammy, wasn't I?"

"Jammy?"

"You know—outrageously lucky. Here I was, on the job no more than ten minutes, and the first gent through the door makes a purchase."

I looked at the cash in my hand. It wouldn't make a dent in Consuela's medical bills, but it would keep the lights on.

The young woman from Acoma who makes those *ollas* for me also makes ceramic thimbles and cute little coyotes and lizards, but I don't stock them. I don't deal in trinkets.

"Did anyone other than the guy who bought the Acoma *olla* come in?"

"There were a few people who looked about but didn't seem inclined to buy. There were also two people who asked after you."

After I what? I was tempted to say, but I guessed he meant "asked *about* you."

"The first one was a red Indian named Martin."

I winced. "That phrase is considered offensive these days."

"Thank you for telling me. I shall strike it from my vocabulary," he said earnestly.

"And the second person who asked about me?"

"It took a bit of doing to get him to give me his name. Carl Wilkes it is, a dodgy-looking fellow with deep-set eyes and a close-cropped gray beard. Said he hoped to receive a certain pot from you. When I told him you hadn't yet returned, he said perhaps that was a good sign that your hunting trip was successful. You don't strike me as a hunter, Hubie."

"Only for pots. Considering you'll be minding the store, I may as well fill you in on a few things. Carl and I are both pot hunters. He used to sell the ones he dug up when he worked for the Army Corps of Engineers. Now that he's retired, he sometimes gets merchandise from me."

"He seemed quite anxious to get it in this case."

"Yes. He already has a buyer for it. Carl offered me thirty thousand, so the buyer must be willing to pay at least fifty."

"Fifty thousand quid for an old pot?"

"A very old and very rare pot. I'm just as anxious to deliver it to Carl as he is to receive it. That's why it's so frustrating that I had my hands on it."

I told him about my trip south and the frustrating timing of the MP being there with Susannah when I returned with the pot. In his usual fashion, Glad hung on my every word and asked about every detail. He was an eager and rapid learner, and any reservations I might have had about having someone else involved in what had been a solo act for over twenty years began to dissipate.

"Did you clean the windows?" I asked him.

"I thought you were having me on."

"If that means joking, then you're right. Can you mind the place again today? I have some errands to run."

He said he would and I left in the Bronco.

Glad's mention of Carl had me thinking about cancer survivors. Carl beat melanoma and went right back to doing what he's always done. Sharice overcame breast cancer, but it changed her entire life. From aspiring dentist to dental hygienist. From Canada to the United States.

There's an organization in New Mexico that provides free

fly-fishing lessons to survivors of breast cancer. The guys who teach the lessons say the women seem more like sisters than strangers. Evidently, the shared experience creates a bond.

In one of the things on her list—explaining her post-cancer life—Sharice made it clear to me that she doesn't want to bond. She wants to forget. Blot it forever from her memory. Which is probably a good thing. Given her lifestyle and wardrobe, I can't imagine her in waders with a fly rod in one hand and a box of artificial insects in the other.

When I returned that afternoon just before closing time, Glad seemed so jovial that I thought he'd sold another pot. After a few pleasantries, he asked, "Can you recommend someone who could get my store kitted out at a reasonable price?"

"'Kitted out'?"

"Display cases, clothes racks, that sort of thing."

"Yeah, you already met him—Martin. He normally does ironwork, but he's also an excellent carpenter. He helped me set up this place. And he also provides some of the merchandise. The colorful pot behind you on the second shelf was made by his uncle."

"Brilliant. I have another question. Do you mind if I use my shop as a kip and take spit baths until I get sorted?"

How do you answer a question like that?

18

How *did* you answer it?" Susannah asked that evening.

We were at our usual table, margaritas in hand, salsa in the metate, chips at the ready. I'd related my conversation with Glad and told her she was in for 20 percent of the Tompiro money. One sale didn't prove she was right about his minding the store increasing my revenue, but the fact that he made a sale on the first day was a good excuse to give her what she deserved.

If I could get anything to give.

"I told him I couldn't answer that. Then he said, 'Excellent,' and gave me a conspiratorial smile. What do you suppose that means?"

"*Kip, sorted out, spit baths* or the smile?"

"All of the above."

"*Kip* is a nap or sometimes the place where you take it, like crashing on someone's sofa. *Sorted out* means getting organized. So he was asking to sleep in the store you're renting to him until he gets himself organized."

"How do you know all this?"

"I watch a lot of British sitcoms."

"What about the smile?"

"Easy. When you said you couldn't answer his question, he took that to mean it wasn't proper for him to live there, but you were willing to look the other way."

"He was right. It's not a proper place to live. There's a sink and toilet, but no shower or bath."

"That explains the *spit bath* part." She laughed. "I remember during lambing season when we spent days and nights out in the fields. My mother told me to take spit baths. When I asked what that was, she said, 'Take a wet cloth, start at your head and wash down as far as possible. Then start at your feet and wash up as far as possible. Then wait until everyone is out of sight and wash 'possible.'"

"Did you sleep on the ground around a campfire and eat beans and bacon for every meal?"

"We did sleep on the ground, but our chuck wagon had a lot more than beans and bacon."

I was trying to decide if she was kidding about the chuck wagon when Martin Seepu joined us and waved for Angie.

"I came to celebrate your sale of the Acoma *olla*," he said to me. Then he said to Angie, "Bring me a Tecate and a bowl of guacamole, and put it on his tab."

"How did you know I sold that *olla*?"

"It was gone when I dropped in for a powwow."

"*Powwow* is a Narragansett word."

"Yeah, but I like the sound of it. Like the beer too, but not as much as Tecate."

I thought I saw a hint of a smile.

Susannah said, "I'm surprised a man would notice one little pot missing."

"Native American man," he added. "We are more attuned to our surroundings."

"That's because there is so little in your surroundings to be attuned to," I said. The land the federal government allowed Martin's tribe to retain is acreage no one wanted, mostly devoid of fertile soil.

"You're right. That is why our tribe invented the saying 'Less is more.'"

"Really?" asked Susannah.

"Yes. It helps us feel good about you whites taking most of our land."

After Angie brought his Tecate and guacamole, Martin looked me over and said, "You took a long walk yesterday searching for pots, and you also worked with clay mortar."

I plopped down my margarita and turned to Susannah. "You told him, right?"

Martin said, "She was with you during the adventure."

Now it was Susannah's turn to plunk down her drink. "What are you—some kind of skin-walking Sherlock?"

"Elementary, my dear paleface. Your skin is tinged pink from too much sun. I saw Carl Wilkes come out of your store, so I figure he has a buyer and wants you to get the pot."

"And my working with clay mortar?"

"Your fingers are dyed from clay."

"That could be from my potting clay."

"Wrong color clay."

"I'm amazed," said Susannah, "and impressed."

"Don't get carried away," I said. "He may know dirt, but he wouldn't last a day in a food court."

"Neither would you," she said, and we all laughed.

I met Martin Seepu when an uncharacteristic impulse to be a do-gooder stirred me to volunteer for a program run by the university that matched college students with reservation adolescents in need of tutoring and maybe a little mentoring. Sort of Big Brothers meets Teach for America.

Martin was a fourteen-year-old dropout. I quickly discovered he had dropped out from boredom rather than lack of academic ability. I was an undergraduate math major at the time, so I tutored him in math even though he wasn't in school and had no intention of returning. When I warned him that number theory has no practical application, I had to explain to him what that meant. It was the only lesson he ever struggled with. Neither his tribe's language nor their metaphysics contains a distinction between practical and theoretical. Knowledge is simply knowledge.

When I got arbitrarily and unjustly kicked out of graduate school for taking pots that it was absolutely and totally legal to take at the time (not that it bothers me anymore), I decided to become a pottery merchant. Martin was a nineteen-year-old five-foot-six-inch stump of muscle by that time. He helped me turn my derelict building into a shop and residence. I asked him if he was interested in doing the same for Glad.

"What does he need done?"

"He said he wanted the place *kitted out*. Glad's a nice guy, but he really needs to learn how to speak English."

"He *is* English," said Susannah. "It's *his* language. We're the ones who don't speak it properly."

I shook my head. "We booted them out two hundred years ago. If he's going to live here, he needs to speak *our* language."

"That's what we should have told the Pilgrims," said Martin. "But we learned English instead and look where that got us."

"Kitted out means fixed up, fully equipped," said Susannah.

"Sure," said Martin, "I can do that. How much is he paying?"

"He said he wanted someone who would do it at a reasonable price."

"Sounds like another case of working for beads, but I'll talk to him."

I saw Glad approaching our table from over Martin's shoulder. Actually, he was approaching from the door—it was just my vision that was over Martin's shoulder.

"You can do it now," I said to Martin, and to Glad, "Please join us. I'll stand you a drink."

Martin said, "'Stand you a drink'?"

"It's real English for 'buy you one.'"

Glad took a seat and said, "As Oscar Wilde said, 'We are two nations divided by a common language.'"

"I thought that was Churchill."

"I thought it was George Bernard Shaw," Susannah said.

Glad shook his head. "Definitely Wilde. Wrote something like it in *The Canterville Ghost* in 1887, but I don't doubt that both Shaw and Churchill said something similar. A long list of people have paraphrased it."

"I'll add to that list," said Martin. "We are one people resisting a common language."

"I say we haven't been properly introduced. I'm Gladwyn Farthing, but people call me Glad."

"My English name is Martin."

They shook hands awkwardly.

"English name. So you have another one in your native tongue?"

Martin nodded and took a sip of Tecate.

After an awkward moment of silence, Glad said, "Did I say something cheeky?"

Before anyone could respond, Angie arrived to take Glad's order.

"I'll have a pink gin," he said.

"I don't think we have that brand."

"It's not a brand—it's a color," he said.

"All our gin is clear except for the Hendricks, which has a green tint because of the cucumbers."

"Sorry. I seem to have made a complete bollocks of my order. What I want is a few ounces of gin with a splash of bitters, no ice and by all means no cucumbers."

Angie smiled and said, "You're actually going to drink that?"

Susannah ordered a second margarita, Martin stopped with the one Tecate as he usually does, and we all laughed as we talked about drink names and English phrases.

The next day was Saturday, and one of my informal scouts had told me there might be some special Indian pottery on the tables at the big flea market at the State Fairgrounds. I pulled Glad aside as we were all leaving and told him I would probably require his shop minding three or four times a month. But for this month, the three days would be consecutive since I wanted to go to the flea market.

19

The second reason I didn't want to mind the shop on Saturday was I had a date with Sharice.

"Adam Lippes," she said, anticipating my question as I stared at the silk blouse with cut-in shoulders.

"Sounds English."

"American. He got his start with Oscar de la Renta."

"Finally a designer I've actually heard of. And the jeans?"

"Another designer you've probably heard of—Levi Strauss."

She uncorked a bottle of Gruet Blanc de Noir and slid it into an ice bucket, a phrase that hardly does justice to the shimmering Nambé cylinder on her table. Benz leapt onto the table and sniffed at the Gruet. Then he rubbed his nose with a paw. The bubbles probably tickled.

"Tonight we're having arctic char."

"Which is what—burned polar bear?"

She giggled. "It's fish. I'm going to sauté it in blood orange *suprêmes* and cognac."

"You sound so sexy speaking French."

"You'd say the same thing if I spoke Míkmaq."

"Or paddywhack, whatever that is."

"It's a nuchal ligament in the neck of a sheep."

"Probably not as tasty as arctic char. And you know about this knuckle ligament how?"

"Not knuckle—*nuchal*. We dissected sheep necks in dental school. Easier to get than human necks."

"Can we change the subject?"

"Sure—kiss me."

I did. Enthusiastically. Images of sheep necks vanished.

Suprêmes turned out to be sections of the orange with the membranes removed. I asked her if blood orange membranes taste bad.

"No, but they're a bit tough."

Probably not as tough as nuchal ligaments, I thought.

The arctic char was spectacular, similar to the coho salmon from New Mexico's El Vado Lake. Yes, there are salmon in New Mexico, and the ones stocked in El Vado flourish because of the cool deep water. Which makes no sense because *vado* means ford, and I don't think you can ford something 150 feet deep.

The only dish other than the char was a slaw of thinly sliced apples and matchstick carrots in a vinaigrette of blood orange juice, grainy mustard and avocado oil.

Eating Sharice's cooking is like dining on another planet. Consuela raised me on chiles rellenos, posole, frijoles and enchiladas both red and green. The only fish we had was on Fridays.

Just a few years before Consuela was hired to be my nanny and my family's cook and housekeeper, Vatican II released Catholics from meatless Fridays. Consuela evidently believed the new policy was heresy.

And who could blame her?

It was 1962. The Supreme Court ruled that mandatory prayer in public schools is unconstitutional. Yet another nuclear bomb was detonated in the atmosphere, this time in Nevada rather than New Mexico. Yet the only issue Vatican II seemed interested in was eating meat on Friday. No wonder Consuela chose to ignore them.

Although I'm not Catholic, I also abstain from meat on Fridays. When I was in high school, the cafeteria served bean burritos for lunch every Friday even though that was long after Vatican II. I like to honor that tradition.

I like trout because it's fresh and local, but Sharice's arctic char was the first thing I'd eaten from the ocean since an unfortunate incident with some mussels about ten years ago. I should have known better than to order moules marinières at a place named Chuy's Mexican Mariscos.

We had blackberries for dessert. When Benz saw us selecting Scrabble tiles and putting them on our stands, he evidently thought the object of the game was to see who could collect the most tiles. He tried to help Sharice win by knocking my tiles off the stand.

After the third time, we switched to the autological word game. Sharice chose *w* as the letter.

"Wee," I said after a couple of minutes.

"Word," she said immediately.

"I can't believe I didn't think of that one." After a few moments, I said, "Whole."

"Wussy," she said without hesitation.

"Showoff."

"Not really. I just have a lot of time to think of my next one because it takes you so long."

"Oh yeah? How about this—wide."

She imitated the sound of a buzzer. "*Wide* is not wide."

"Sure it is—*w* is a very wide letter."

"Nice try, but there is no way I'm ruling a four-letter word to be wide."

"Okay, I'll find another."

I thought about *wing*, but the word itself has no wings. Then inspiration struck. All I had to do was negate the word.

"Wingless."

"Writable."

"Witless."

"Which describes your new strategy. You're just going to append *-less* to everything. Okay, two can play at that game. Weaponless."

"Wartless."

"Yuk. Wageless."

"Wakeless."

"Waveless."

"Weedless."

"Wishless."

"Womanless," I said.

She smiled. "I'll bet you've never been womanless."

"I have. Most of my life, in fact. But being with you now more than compensates."

While I smiled at her like a witless teenager, she seemed absorbed in thought. She asked me if I remembered the scene in *Four Weddings and a Funeral* where Hugh Grant and Andie MacDowell tell each other about their sexual histories.

A warning bell clanged in my mind. "Not in detail."

"I think we should do that."

"Uh . . . I'm not sure that's a good idea. Why bring up stuff from the past? Actually, I don't have much of a past. And nothing from your past would change how I feel about you, so—"

"It's one of those things I have to do, Hubie."

"Your one-at-a-time list?"

She nodded. "You go first."

I swallowed. It was so loud, people in the next apartment probably heard it.

"The last woman I had a relationship with was Dolly Aguirre. She was the daughter of my history teacher at Albuquerque High School."

"Wow. You knew her from high school? Sounds serious."

"I didn't know her in high school. She was a freshman when I was a senior. We didn't meet until a couple of years ago." A possible exit from this conversation occurred to me. "It turns out she had been divorced three times. When she told me that, it didn't bother me at all. So that sort of makes my point that there really is no purpose in us telling each other about—"

She was shaking her head. "We have to do this. *I* have to do this."

So I did. It was perhaps the most uncomfortable three minutes of my life.

Yes—three minutes. Well, what did you expect? I already admitted I've been womanless most of my life. Plus, I kept details to a minimum.

"So I guess it's my turn," she said.

"You don't have to—"

"Yes, I do."

We looked at each other in silence for perhaps thirty seconds.

"Okay," she said, "I'm finished."

"You didn't say anything."

"I said everything there was to say on the topic."

Another few seconds passed in silence.

"So you have nothing to tell me?"

She nodded.

"So does that mean . . . ?" I let the question hang in the air.

"It does."

"You're a . . ."

"I am."

The next five seconds took five minutes to elapse.

"Surprised?"

"Yes. You're impossibly attractive and fun to be around. And I know from sleeping with you on our last date that you are obviously not frigid."

She laughed.

"What's so funny?"

"That may be the first time any man ever said 'sleeping with' to actually mean sleeping with. The fact is I'm as surprised about my virginity as you are. It's not like I planned it. I was admitted to dental school when I was nineteen. You can start in Canada before you have a baccalaureate. I figured my first experience would be with some handsome and charming dentist in training. I had no idea what dental school was like. The only way a guy would take time out from studying to court me was if he thought it would distract me enough to lower my grades. I couldn't believe how competitive they were. And conceited."

She paused to sip some Gruet. I thought that was an excellent idea and did the same.

Benz jumped onto my lap. He weighs as much as Geronimo, but he's lighter on his feet. "I guess he *does* like me."

"He sees me talking to you, so he jumped up there to be in my line of sight."

"Oh."

She swallowed. "Then I found the lump."

I rubbed Benz behind the ears. He started purring.

"Fast-forward to the new me living in a dark apartment on San Mateo with no furniture, no friends, no designer dresses and no left breast. I worked all day and saved my money for the operation. But every penny I dropped in the piggy bank made me sadder. One day closer to another operation. Never mind that it was giving me something rather than taking something away. It still involved hospital, surgery, pain and fear."

She bit her lip. A teardrop teetered. "I need to tell you something scary."

"Another thing on the list?"

"Yes. And another one we are never to speak of again." She took a deep breath. "In addition to saving pennies, I started saving midazolam."

"That's a semiprecious stone like agate, right?"

She didn't laugh at my lame joke.

"Dentists use it for sedation. Florida used it to execute William Happ."

"Oh." Something twitched in my stomach.

"A woman named Angie Crowley stopped at a convenience store to use a pay phone. Happ smashed her car window and kidnapped her. After raping her, he strangled her with her stretch pants and threw her body in a canal."

I swallowed hard. "Sounds like Florida put the drug to good use."

"I had enough for another execution."

I stared into those green eyes. "I'm glad you didn't use it."

"I almost did. Then I thought about my parents. I couldn't do that to them. I decided a happy life is a lot more important than a breast." She paused and smiled. "Especially one made from butt tissue."

After we stopped laughing, she said, "I flushed the midazolam. I used my operation money for a down payment on this condo. I traded shag carpet, Formica and harvest gold for polished concrete, granite and stainless steel. I gave my clothes to Goodwill. I bought designer dresses and expensive perfumes. I made myself beautiful again. Then I started dating."

"And men from the four corners of the Earth celebrated."

"Right. Until I told them I don't have—"

"I thought we were never to talk about that."

She cried for a few moments—smiling while doing so—then regained her composure. "If it got to the stage where I liked them enough, I told them. They all said it didn't matter. Then they stopped calling."

"Glad they did. Otherwise you might not have been available for me."

"I suspected right from the start that you were the one. The man who would like me despite—"

"There is no *despite*. There is nothing to get over or learn to deal with. It's not like you keep a glass eye in a jar of water on your nightstand."

"I think maybe your sense of humor is what made me think you wouldn't run away. When you made light of my dramatic moment by hoisting your ankle onto my bed, it was the happiest moment of my life."

"It was the *second* happiest moment of my life."

"What was the happiest one?"

"It hasn't happened yet."

She blushed. Which was interesting to watch, given her complexion.

"And it won't happen tonight," she said.

First the neighbors heard me swallow. Now they heard me sigh. "Why not?" I asked, trying not to sound petulant.

"It's too soon after the bombshell I just dropped on you. You need some time to think about it. But you can sleep over if you still want to."

We had been asleep only an hour or so when Susannah called to tell me her car had died on the way back from La Reina.

Sharice said, "You can't leave her stranded all night."

"You're right, but this is only the second night we've slept together."

Her giggle is childlike and charming. "That's the second time you've used that phrasing literally. It won't be long until you'll use it metaphorically like everyone else." She kissed me. "Go rescue Susannah."

20

It was well after midnight when I spotted Susannah's Crown Vic on the shoulder of the dirt road south of La Reina.

On the one hand, it's a terrible place to be stranded. Even though Rio Arriba County covers over 5,000 square miles, its county seat, Tierra Amarilla, has only 700 residents and is not even incorporated as a town. There are no all-night convenience stores, no garages open after dark.

On the other hand, it's a good place to be stranded. The chances of anybody being on that dirt road in the wee hours of the night are one in a million. The odds against that one being a threat are even higher.

Abiquiú, the village where Georgia O'Keeffe spent the last thirty-five years of her life, is also in Rio Arriba County, about forty-five miles southeast of Tierra Amarilla. It's a bigger town—almost 1,000 people. Nothing open after dark.

You might die of loneliness, but not from violence.

It was not always so.

O'Keeffe had been in the county almost twenty years when the Alianza Federal de Mercedes, led by Reies Tijerina, raided the Rio Arriba County Courthouse. The Alianza claimed the land grants given to the original Spanish settlers of the area were valid under the Treaty of Guadalupe Hidalgo between the United States and Mexico.

Tijerina's cause was probably just, but his actions were bizarre. In October of 1966, he and his group (mostly descendants of the original grant holders) occupied Echo Amphitheater Park in the Carson National Forest and proclaimed it the Republic of San Joaquín del Rio de Chama. They issued visas to the surprised tourists who stopped in. When forest rangers tried to remove the squatters, Tijerina arrested them. They were tried, convicted of trespassing, given suspended sentences and released without harm other than to their dignity.

Some of Tijerina's colleagues were arrested for this activity. The raid on the courthouse freed them and made Tijerina famous for fifteen minutes.

Imprisoned several times, he led a colorful and bizarre life. On the day in 1969 when Warren Burger was sworn in as Chief Justice of the Supreme Court, Tijerina went to Washington to place him under citizen's arrest. Burger dodged the arrest by exiting out a back door.

Maybe growing up in a state colonized by Spain rather than England and by people who were granted land a century before the Pilgrims hit Plymouth Rock explains why I don't have any qualms about ignoring the Archaeological Resources Protection Act. Politicians and bureaucrats back east are clueless about New Mexico. Trying to arrest them is charmingly quixotic, but I'll just stick to ignoring them.

I found Susannah on the hood of the Crown Vic gazing up at the heavens.

"What are those two?" she asked, pointing.

I arched my back and followed the line of her finger. "That one is Sirius."

"It looks frivolous."

"The one next to it is Canis Major."

"They're so bright."

"Yep. One of the best things about living here is the high altitude and dry air make you feel like you can reach up and grab a handful of stars. See that fainter line of stars below Canis Major running parallel to the horizon? The Navajo say those are the tracks of a celestial rabbit."

"You don't even need a telescope out here."

New Mexico has one of the strongest night-sky protection laws in the country. It helps in Albuquerque, but it isn't needed out here on a dirt road west of the Jemez Mountains, where it can seem like Thomas Edison was never born.

"What's wrong with your car?"

"It keeps stalling. I think the throttle position sensor is broken."

"I don't know what that is, but obviously you can't fix it or you wouldn't have called me. Do you just want a ride back to Albuquerque or do you want me to tow your car back?"

"I'd rather tow it now than have you make another trip."

We hooked my tow rope under the Crown Vic's bumper. I would have enjoyed her company, but she had to ride in her car and use the brakes to keep it from running into me when I slowed or stopped.

"Good thing the stars are so bright," she said. "I'm not turning my headlights on. I don't want a dead battery on top of a dead sensor."

Once we got rolling, it was all downhill, so the tug I felt was not Susannah's car. It was the memory of Sharice saying I had to give more thought to her virginity before—excuse the phrase—taking the plunge.

But why? The only answer I could come up with is that doing the deed carried a commitment of some sort. That conjured up my high school friend Naldo stammering and sweating as he explained that his cousin and her girlfriend from Portales were coming to Albuquerque because they wanted to have sex before they went to college, and was I interested in pairing with his cousin. I had only the vaguest idea about the mechanics of the operation, but what I lacked in experience I made up for in enthusiasm.

Our pooled money was just enough to cover dinner for four at La Hacienda and a room at a cheap hotel on Central. We flipped a coin. I got the room. He got the backseat of the car. His cousin—I feel bad that I can't remember her name—did not strike me as the sort of young woman who would drive two hundred miles to have sex with a stranger. We were both so nervous when I closed the door to the motel room that the floor was vibrating. We kissed awkwardly. Since my arms were already around her, I seized the moment to unzip her dress. She stepped back and let it fall to the floor.

I hadn't anticipated her full slip, which was like a second dress. She lay down on the bed. I removed my jacket and tie and lay beside her. I suspected that actually having sex would require shedding a lot more of our garments, but I took her dress and my jacket and tie as a good start.

We resumed kissing. My left hand groped awkwardly under her clothes. She let it roam around aimlessly for a moment, then gently pushed it away. "Can I ask you a question?"

"Sure."

"When you get married, do you want your wife to be a virgin?"

I'd never had a girlfriend, much less given thought to whom I might marry. What I *did* have an opinion about was my own sexual status. I was anxious *not* to be a virgin.

Her query seemed like a trick question to thwart my objective.

One of the drawbacks of insecurity is the tendency to over-analyze. She wouldn't have sex with me if I said yes because what I hoped to do with her would disqualify her from marrying any-one who gave the answer I gave. And she wouldn't have sex with me if I said no because she knew that's why I was there, and who wants to have sex with a liar?

So I fell back on the ploy of answering a question with a ques-tion. "When you get married, do you want your husband to be a virgin?"

"I don't know."

"Okay," I said, hoping for the best, "that's my answer too."

It didn't work. We had a friendly conversation. We smooched a bit more. But she was unwilling to risk sex while the conse-quences of doing so were uncertain.

But we're not only in a new century, we're in a new millen-nium. The sexual revolution took place before I was even born. Sex won. Surely Sharice wasn't intimating that I had to make some sort of commitment before having sex with her. In the first place, I was already committed. In the second place . . .

I never got to the second place, because some idiot behind me started honking. A glance into the rearview mirror revealed the silhouette of a vehicle with no lights. Obviously a drunk or a runaway with no brakes—the guy was only a dozen feet behind me. I feared he was so out of control that he might rear-end me at any moment.

The Bronco began to buck. I looked ahead and saw I'd run onto the shoulder while looking into the mirror.

I managed to wrestle the Bronco back onto the road just in time to see the stop sign where the dirt road intersected the main highway. Slamming on the brakes catapulted me forward. After a loud crashing sound, I was thrust rearward as the out-of-control no-lights vehicle slammed into me. And had the nerve to keep honking.

Then I realized it was my own horn, jammed into the honk position by the force of the collision.

I know full well that after a collision, the drivers of the cars involved are supposed to pull off the road, call the police and wait until an officer arrives.

I wondered if there were an exception in cases where the person who ran into you might be a crazed druggie. I was about to floor the accelerator and race to the next town, horn blaring, when the strangest thing happened.

Susannah stepped out of the car that had rammed me.

21

We didn't get back to Albuquerque until six in the morning, so I was not happy when Detective Whit Fletcher banged on my door at eight.

"You look like hell, Hubert."

"It's Sunday morning, Whit. I normally sleep late on Sundays."

"You sleep late every morning. I reckon you musta just got home after spending the night with that colored woman you been dating."

"Jeez, Whit. Saying something like that could get you kicked off the force."

"What's wrong with it? Even those liberals on public radio call them *women of color*."

"*Woman of color* and *colored woman* are completely different."

"Yeah, the words are in a different order. Big deal. I remember when *black* was an insult. I don't try too hard to keep up with what's politically correct. Which I guess makes me the wrong guy to have to tell you the bad news. I'll just give it to you straight— Carl Wilkes was shot to death yesterday."

"I didn't do it."

"I know that, Hubert."

"Yeah, and you knew it when you arrested me last year."

"There was a warrant. I was just doing my duty. But no one is accusing you this time."

I know it doesn't reflect well on my character that my first thought on hearing that Carl was dead was selfish—hoping I wasn't a suspect. But I had a legitimate reason to be worried. When I've been accused of murder—which is less often than Whitey Bulger but more often than the average citizen—it's always Fletcher who breaks the news.

In a way, that's good. He knows I'm not capable of murder, and he's helped me exonerate myself. Whit and I have also shared a few bucks that we came by in unorthodox ways. Like the time a pot that was evidence in a crime found its way into my shop and we split the sales price. The crime in question was the murder of the pot's owner, who had no heirs, and Whit figured it was an inefficient use of resources to leave a valuable Anasazi in the evidence locker. He's otherwise a good cop and cares more about murderers than he does about pot thieves.

"You aren't a suspect. You ain't even a person of interest." He laughed derisively at the phrase. "What I want is help. You're the only person we know who knew him. Did he have any enemies you know about, stuff like that?"

"He never mentioned any enemies."

"You talk to him lately?"

"Yeah. He wanted me to get him a certain kind of pot. I was working on it."

"How much was he going to pay for it?"

"Thirty thousand."

He whistled in appreciation. "Maybe you should keep working on getting that pot."

"It won't do me much good now that Carl is dead. He never told me who his buyer was."

"'Course not. Probably afraid you might cut out the middleman. But my investigation might turn up the name of the buyer. I could share that information with you for a cut of the proceeds."

"Be careful. The buyer might be the murderer."

"You'd make a lousy cop, Hubert. If the buyer was gonna kill Wilkes, he would've done it *after* he got the pot."

That made sense, of course, but the murder could still be related somehow to the Tompiro pot deal, and that made me nervous.

After Whit left, my thoughts turned belatedly to Carl's death. Should I feel guilty that my initial reaction was concern over whether I was a suspect? That I didn't think to ask about services? That I didn't know whether he had family?

In my first lesson with Martin, I directed him to draw a straight line on a piece of paper and then add a dot anywhere away from the line.

"How many lines can pass through the dot and be parallel to the line?" I asked him.

Remember, he was fourteen years old. He probably had the rudiments of plane geometry before he dropped out of school, so he knew what parallel meant, but I doubt his seventh-grade geometry teacher dealt with the subtleties of Euclid.

"Just one," he said.

"How did you come to that answer?"

He looked at the paper rather than at me as he explained. "I imagined a parallel line through the dot. I could see that if you rotate it in either direction it wouldn't be parallel."

He was right, of course. Euclid's famous Fifth Postulate, the one Martin could see was true, is obvious to anyone who thinks about it. But it cannot be proved. That's why Euclid called it a postulate—a starting point that you accept as true because it's so obvious.

Why am I nattering along about the Fifth Postulate and what has it to do with Carl Wilkes's death? Well, there is a similar postulate about death. When someone you know dies, you need to *do something*. That's just as obvious to me as Euclid's postulate. And just as impossible to prove.

What I *don't* know is what to do. Send flowers? Light a candle? Make a donation to the deceased's favorite charity?

I usually end up doing whatever everyone else is doing because not doing so seems disrespectful. If there's a funeral, I go. If there's a memorial service, I go. If there's a dispersal of ashes, I go. I even attended an event where everyone was required to compose a spontaneous haiku in honor of the dearly departed, and I managed to both come up with a haiku and keep a straight face.

I'd had two hours of sleep. Thinking about Carl's murder and death in general was depressing me. I put my CLOSED FOR THE DAY sign on the door and went back to bed.

22

⁓

Are you still mad at me for causing us to crash?"

"No. But I'm still mad that you won't tell me why you were so distracted."

"I *did* tell you."

"Saying you were lost in thought is not telling me anything, Hubert. Telling me would be saying what you were thinking *about*."

What I don't tell Susannah of my own volition, she usually drags out of me. I kind of like when she does that. But I couldn't tell her about Sharice's "bombshell" because some things can't be shared even with your best friend. So being unable to mollify Susannah, I changed the subject and told her about Carl and my vacillation, both of thought and action.

She lofted her margarita and said, "To Carl Wilkes."

"It's not a funeral, memorial service or dispersal of ashes," I said, clinking my glass against hers, "but at least it's something."

"And better than spontaneous haikus. Did you really attend an event like that or did you just make it up?"

"You can't make up something like that."

I recited one of the poems I remembered:

A rippling trout stream —
A rainbow's lips strike the nymph
The fisherman smiles

"Doesn't sound like funeral material."

"The dead guy loved trout fishing."

"What was your haiku?"

"I don't remember."

She leaned over and looked under the table. "Just trying to see if your pants are on fire."

"Okay, I do remember."

A six-foot wood box
Floating across the river Styx
Fish therein rejoice

She frowned. "So in addition to joining me in a toast to a guy I hardly knew, what else are you going to do?"

"Like I just said, I have no idea."

"In one of the Bernie Rhodenbarr books, Bernie's partner is killed. Bernie says, 'When your partner is killed, you have to do something about it. Maybe he was not a good partner, and you didn't like him much, but that doesn't matter. He was your partner, and you're supposed to do something about it.'"

"That line came from *The Maltese Falcon*."

"Really? Well, it doesn't matter who said it first. The point is you have to do something about it."

"Carl was not my partner."

"He was partner enough for you to illegally dig up an old pot on the White Sands Missile Range when there was thirty thousand in it for you. But now that he's dead, it's like you hardly knew him. Clink a glass in his name and move on."

"He wasn't my partner, but at least I liked him. Which is more than you can say for Sam Spade and his partner, Miles Archer. Spade had an affair with Archer's wife, not a very partnerly thing to do. I wouldn't have cavorted with Carl's wife if he had one."

"And especially if he didn't have one."

"Right. I'll do something. I just don't know what."

"Not to sound mercenary, but I guess my twenty percent of that pot died along with Carl."

"Maybe not. Whit thinks his investigation may turn up the name of the buyer."

"Let me guess—he gets a cut."

"Of course. But even after your share and his cut, it's enough to pay off most of my debts. But first we have to get the pot."

I swear it was like she knew I was going to say that, and she already had it all worked out.

"We can do that next week during the Annual Bataan Death March Memorial."

"Shouldn't that be the Bataan Death March Annual Memorial? Because, thankfully, the Bataan Death March doesn't happen every year, just the memorial to it."

"Are you going to quibble about word order, or do you want to hear the plan?"

"Is it long and complicated?"

"Sort of. You want to get a refill first?"

I said I did. When Angie had us reprovisioned, I said, "The Memorial March is on the wrong end of the range."

Susannah pulled a brochure from her backpack. "Not this year. Something to do with top-secret maneuvers involving the

F-22A Stealth Fighters at Holloman near the south entrance. So they moved the event farther north for this one year. An omen, right?"

"Right. But is it a good one or a bad one?"

"You say you're an optimist, so let's assume it's a good one. The location has changed, but the entrance procedures haven't. They're stricter than the Trinity Site event, probably because the participants won't be going straight in and straight out."

"They'll go in and out crooked?"

She shook her head. "They'll go around in circles. One route is twenty-six miles, a marathon. The other route is only fourteen. The routes overlap because the twenty-sixers have to make part of one loop twice and both routes pass not too far from where you buried the pot."

"In that case, I'll choose the fourteen-mile route."

"No. We'll choose the long one, but we won't actually do it."

When I started to question her, she held up a palm and continued. "People who do the twenty-six miles are hardcore. They go first and they don't lollygag. So it's easy to fall to the back of the group and eventually be far enough behind that no one notices us leaving the road. We dig up the pot, return to the road and fall in with the fourteen-milers, the twenty-six milers on their second pass or whatever stragglers happen to be there."

"What if the officials notice that we started with the twenty-sixers and finished with the fourteeners?"

"There were over five thousand participants last year. I don't think they pay any attention to what group you finish in. And even if they do, we can just say you ran out of gas, and I stayed with you out of loyalty."

"Swell."

"There is one problem though. They search backpacks, handbags and other stuff going in and coming out."

"Not a problem," I said smugly, "I'll use the museum ploy."

"You can make a fake that quickly?"

"Sure. It won't need glazing, I won't need to mix colors and the design is straight lines."

23

The next morning, I asked Glad to watch the shop and not interrupt me. Once my hands are in clay, I like to stick with the job.

I normally use sheets of clay to make replicas—the ancients didn't have pottery wheels. But this one wouldn't have to fool a collector, only an MP at the missile range. So I used the wheel to speed things along. After I'd coaxed the clay into shape, I let the wheel spin slowly to a stop. Then I deformed the sides to efface the factory look the wheel had imparted.

I mixed the pigment while the pot dried in the kiln set on low. When it was time to decorate, I re-ran my mental movie of the potter to guide me in placing the hatchings.

It had the wrong sort of clay. It was dried in an electric kiln. It was decorated with commercial pigments rather than natural elements. But to the untrained eye, it looked like the pot I had buried. It would suit my purpose.

But so what? I wasn't proud of it.

O'Keeffe said, "I have always first had a show for myself—and made up my mind—then after that it doesn't matter to me very much what anyone else says—good or bad."

It didn't matter that the pot would fool an MP. I was not satisfied with it.

So I decided to do it the ancient way. I gathered some thin shoots from the cottonwood trees in my patio and wove them into an armature. I rolled out sheets of clay and pressed them onto the frame, wetting my fingers to work the seams together. I built a fire in my clay *horno* and fired the pot as a Tompiro potter would have done.

I mixed limonite and ochre in a metate. I didn't have any willow sap, so I used tap water. Given that the water in Albuquerque comes from the aquifer beneath the Rio Grande, it probably has willow sap in it. Not to mention a lot of other things that shouldn't be in drinking water.

I tossed the first fake into the plastic garbage pail that was half full of empty pigment jars and shards of pots from recently failed firings. There was also an empty bottle of Gruet in there—sometimes I use champagne while working with pots.

I wondered if any of the workers at Gruet do just the opposite—use pot while working with champagne. I can't help it—my mind just works that way.

I expected to hear that sharp crackling sound fired clay makes upon impact, but all I heard was *shusssh*. I'd forgotten that I'd also thrown away an armload of bubble wrap that had protected a pot by the famous Maria of San Ildefonso.

I had popped a few of the bubbles before discarding the sheets. Why do we do that?

I'd bought that pot online from a collector in Houston. Tristan did the online part. All I did was give him my credit card number and expiration date.

Actually, it was the card's expiration date. None of us knows our personal expiration date. Which is definitely a good thing. Given how I obsess over minor things, knowing the date of my death would likely send me into a neurotic stupor.

The expense for the Maria—$8,000 for a small pot—was now on my past-due MasterCard.

I washed up and stepped back to my kitchen to start some vegetarian tacos. I tossed chopped onions and tomatoes into a pan and went to the shop while they sautéed.

"I'm doing some tacos," I said to Glad. "You want some lunch?"

"I just finished. A most delightful woman brought lunch for you. When I told her you were too busy to eat, she insisted I try it, and I did."

"And lived to tell about it. That would be Miss Gladys."

"Yes. I can't work out how a woman with such an engaging personality remains unmarried. Especially one who cooks so well."

"She *was* married. She's a widow."

"But she introduced herself as *miss*."

"She was raised in an area where *miss* is evidently used as a genteel title rather than an indication of marital status. What was the dish?"

"Bubble and squeak, but she didn't call it that."

"I not surprised she didn't. What the devil is bubble and squeak?"

"In England, it's made from the leftovers of a roast dinner. You panfry the veggies. Cabbage and mash, of course, and maybe peas if those were served. You bake it with the brown sauce from the roast. But Miss Claiborne used cans of something called Veg-All and made her own brown sauce by combining ketchup and Worcestershire. Quite inventive, don't you think?"

"Quite."

Gladwyn Farthing was turning out to be a godsend. Not only was he paying rent, he was minding the shop and saving me from eating the casseroles.

I returned to the kitchen and scooped the sautéed onions and tomatoes into tortillas, added diced avocado and chopped fresh cilantro and—mindful of the drinking water in Albuquerque—washed the tacos down with a cold Tecate.

I justified the beer with lunch because I'd be skipping margaritas with Susannah. I had a date that night with Sharice.

24

She cracked the door a few inches. Only her face and left hand were visible.

"Take my hand and close your eyes." She led me through the apartment and back to the bedroom. "You can open your eyes now."

She was naked.

"Love your outfit," I said.

"Glad you do. But you're overdressed for the occasion. Let me help."

She unbuckled my belt. I figured this was the night.

It was.

And that's all I'm going to say about it.

Well, I will say one thing. Just before we jumped into bed, I heard myself say, "Marry me."

When we were dressed, she opened the door to the balcony and let Benz in.

"What was he doing on the balcony?"

"He likes to sit out there and watch the pedestrians." She hesitated before adding, "And I didn't want him in the house while we were . . ."

"Oh."

She opened the oven and extracted something I chose to think of as a one-dish-meal, although it was dangerously close to being a casserole.

"The green chiles are great," I said, "but what are they stuffed with?"

"Porcinis, shallots, cream and cognac."

"Porcinis are little pieces of pork?"

"You know I don't eat meat."

"So I guess that rules out my second guess that they're nuchal ligaments."

She giggled. "They're mushrooms."

They were rich, earthy, complex and delightfully chewy.

The chilled Gruet was the perfect complement to the creamy entrée.

"I guess I can't bring you yuccas anymore."

"Why?"

"They're known here as the candles of the virgin. You no longer qualify."

She laughed as she took away my champagne flute. "No more for you just yet." She flashed that wanton smile. "Champagne, that is."

She put Benz back on the balcony.

25

My plan the next day was to sit in the shop uninterrupted by customers and bask in the memory.

And maybe take a nap at some point. I didn't get much sleep.

The plan was thwarted by visitors. They didn't come to buy pots, alas. They came because of Carl Wilkes. News of his death must have reached most of the people who knew him.

The first guy was a square-shouldered fellow with a matching face and a flattop. Which was not merely the name of his hairstyle but an extremely accurate description. It looked as if each hair had been individually cut so that no single strand would differ in length from its colleagues. I wondered how much time he spent in the barber's chair.

"Jack Haggard," he said, extending a hand. "You Hubert Schuze?"

"I am."

"Carl Wilkes told me about you. I guess you know he's dead."

I nodded. His tone matched his appearance—blocky.

"Carl and I were associates," he said.

Now there's a word. *Associates.* Designed to muddy the water. If Jack wanted me to know his relationship with Carl, he would have told me they were business partners, friends, adversaries, neighbors, brothers-in-law, high school teammates.

But they were associates. Which told me only that he didn't want me to know what his connection was with Carl.

He was evidently waiting for me to say what *my* connection was with Carl.

I didn't. I just nodded again.

"Shocking," he said, after he realized I wasn't going to speak.

"Yes, it was."

"When's the last time you saw him?"

"Are you a policeman, Mr. Haggard?"

"No, no."

"Because the police asked me when I had seen him and what we talked about and other things like that as part of their investigation. And since it's an ongoing investigation, I don't think I should talk about it with anyone at this point."

"I see," he said, although he obviously didn't. "That's too bad. I was hoping you could help me."

"In what way?"

"Carl and I were working on something. A deal."

"Oh." He and Carl were *associates* and they were working on a *deal*. The man was a font of information.

"It was a deal that involved, uh . . . your profession."

"You two were going to open a retail shop?"

He looked disappointed. "No. The deal involved you, I believe."

"Hmm."

"He tell you a name of someone else maybe it involved?"

"Sorry, but I really can't talk about it."

"It's important to me," he said.

"I can't help you."

"What if I wrote it down?"

"Wrote it down?"

He extracted a card from his shirt pocket, wrote on it and handed it to me.

He had written one word—*tompiro*.

"Well," he said, "what do you think?"

"I think that word should be capitalized."

He frowned. He took the card back and wrote on it again. He handed it back to me. "Think it over, then call me. There may be big money in it for you."

After he left, I looked at the card. The side he wrote on was white and matte like ordinary paper. Which explains why he could write on it. In addition to *tompiro* there was a phone number with a 915 area code. The only two area codes in New Mexico are 505 and 575.

The other side of the card was high-gloss yellow with equally shiny black lettering that read: ACE BAIL BONDS, RELIABLE 24-HOUR SERVICE.

Not to be snooty, but the use of all capital letters did not strike me as a sign of reliability. The telephone number for Ace Bail Bonds had a 575 area code.

Maybe the deal Haggard mentioned that he and Carl were working on was starting a bail-bond company.

Maybe Jack's nickname was Ace, and he was Carl's preferred bail bondsman. Or maybe Jack was the one who needed the services of a bail bondsman.

There were, no doubt, other possibilities, but I didn't explore them because I heard the bong and looked up to see a couple entering Spirits in Clay hand in hand.

A flap on the back of the man's forest-green shirt ran between his shoulder blades. I suppose the idea is to provide ventilation. But when the ambient temperature is higher than normal body temperature—as it frequently is in Albuquerque—the air drawn in will increase your heat rather than lower it. His twill pants were held up by a belt whose buckle was partially hidden under a pouch any marsupial would be proud of.

The woman wore cargo shorts and a pink shirt, also vented. They looked like a couple of tourists on the type of safari where you view lions from the windows of air-conditioned buses.

"You must be Hubert Schultz," she said. "We're the Edwardses—Donald and Dotty. Carl Wilkes was our dear friend. He often spoke of you. When we found out he was dead, I said, 'Donald'"—she looked at him and he nodded to affirm that she had indeed addressed him—"we just *must* visit Mr. Schultz to convey our deepest sympathies."

She turned to him and he nodded again.

"Actually, my name is Schuze, not Schultz."

Dotty clasped her hands in front of her. "I am sooo sorry. I'm just terrible with names. Donald will tell you that." She looked at Donald and he nodded. "I tell you, Mr. Chews, when it comes to names, my memory is a sieve. And of course it's worse in times of pressure like this."

I didn't know if the pressure was from the death of their dear friend Carl, from her mixing up my name or from the warm air that must have been streaming up through her vented shirt.

When I didn't say anything, she continued. "Carl was not only a friend, he was a scout."

"A Boy Scout?"

She giggled nervously. "Isn't that funny, Donald?" Another look, another nod. "What I meant to say is that he found things for us."

"Old things," Donald said.

"Right," Dotty added, "*very* old things. Our entire house is decorated with *very old things*."

Donald cleared his throat. "You see, Hubert—you don't mind if we call you Hubert, do you?" It must have been a rhetorical question because he didn't pause long enough for me to answer. "We love the ancient peoples of this land. We study them."

"We have a library full of books about the ancient ones, don't we, Donald?"

"We do, and three other rooms just for our collections."

"Large rooms," said Dotty, "packed full of ancient treasures."

"And Carl helped you find those treasures."

"You *do* understand. What did I say, Donald? Didn't I say he would understand?" She continued after Donald nodded. "I said, 'Donald, anyone who was such a good friend of Carl's will understand.' I just knew it."

They smiled at me. After thirty seconds or so, I decided they expected me to say something. "Thank you for coming by. I suspect Carl would be happy that you did."

"Excellent," she said.

"Great," he said.

"So we can expect to hear from you?" she asked.

"When the time and circumstances are appropriate," I replied.

Donald handed me his card, and they left.

His card was a staid, low-sheen white on both sides even though there was lettering only on one—his name and phone number with only the first letters of his Christian and family names capitalized.

26

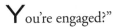

Y ou're engaged?"

"No."

"But you just said you asked her to marry you. Don't tell me she said no."

Having spent the night with Sharice and part of the day with Jack Haggard and the Edwardses, I had plenty of fodder for the cocktail hour.

"She didn't say no," I answered, "and she didn't say yes."

"She said maybe?"

I shook my head. "She didn't say anything. She just laughed. Then she pulled me into bed and . . . well."

"I know—you *consummated* your relationship. Congratulations, by the way. What's it been? Three years since your first date? Call Guinness—they probably want you in their book."

"Three years ago wasn't a date. It was just lunch. And most of the time we've been dating, I've been in one cast followed by another."

"Equivocations and excuses. Admit it, Hubert, this courtship has been positively Victorian. I know you won't give details, but can you at least say something about it?"

"Sure. It was worth the wait."

Her shoulders slumped. "I could tell that from the dopey smile you showed up with tonight. Can't you just share a little romantic something about it?"

"Okay. She asked me to close my eyes while I was still standing outside her front door. Then she took me by the hand and led me to the bedroom. When I opened my eyes, she was completely naked."

She laughed. "I love it. No points for being coy, but I admire the girl's take-charge attitude. So after you did the deed, she just pretended you hadn't proposed to her?"

"She must have thought I was joking."

"Why would she think that?"

"Maybe she thought I was using humor to express my delight. You know—she's standing there in her birthday suit about to drag me into bed, and instead of saying *Thank you* or *I'm really excited about this*, I say *Marry me*."

"So you *were* joking?"

I sipped my margarita. "I don't know. I just blurted it out. Maybe I subconsciously wanted to propose."

She sighed. "I'd settle for any proposal—conscious, subconscious or unconscious."

I jumped on that to change the subject. "You want Baltazar to propose to you?"

"It'd be nice to be asked, but I don't know what I'd say. He's a fun guy and a nice person. But he seems rooted in La Reina."

"And you don't want to live there."

"I don't know. Willard is about the same size, but after living in Albuquerque all these years . . ." She paused. "Let's get back to you and Sharice. I know how much you like her. So now that you two are sleeping together and you proposed to her—"

"I didn't propose to her—it just popped out."

"Like you said, it was a subconscious proposal. So what's next—you two going to play house?"

"I don't know. Do people shack up these days after one night of sex?"

She frowned. "No one says *shack up* anymore. And anyway, you're asking the wrong girl. I've never lived with a man. I would have moved in with Kauffman had he asked me to, but it might have been awkward, since his wife was living with him."

"Don't beat yourself up—you didn't know he was married."

"And I could still move in with Freddie, but only on the days when they allow conjugal visits."

"Not your problem. He hadn't murdered anyone until you started dating him."

"So I turned him into a murderer?"

"Of course not. Look, you've had a bad stretch, but these things even out in the long run. Maybe Baltazar's the one. If not, I'm sure Mr. Right is right around the corner."

Her smile returned. "Of course he is—Mr. Right wouldn't be *left* around the corner." She dipped a chip in the salsa. "So the Haggard guy, he must be a pot hunter."

"Or a bail bondsman."

"Or a pot hunter who keeps a bail bondsman's card just in case. You should do that, Hubie."

"I don't need a bail bondsman. I've been digging up pots for over twenty years and never been arrested."

"I meant for the next time you get arrested for murder."

"Don't even joke about that."

"And Donald and Dotty must be collectors. You know what, Hubie? I'll bet they were in it together."

"In what together?"

"The Tompiro caper."

"Caper?"

"That's exactly what this is. Like *The Maltese Falcon.*"

"How is it like *The Maltese Falcon?*"

"You should remember. You even quoted that line about partners. Peter Lorre offers Humphrey Bogart five thousand for the Maltese falcon, but Bogart doesn't have it. Then Sydney Greenstreet pays him ten thousand for it, but it turns out to be a fake."

"And the similarity is?"

"Carl offered you thirty thousand for a pot, but you didn't have it. Now Haggard also wants it—he even wrote the word on that card."

"He forgot to capitalize it."

"Will you just pay attention? He wants the bird, so you can sell it to him just like Bogart sold it to Greenstreet. But you sell him the fake you made. So he gets a fake just like Greenstreet did."

She looked positively triumphant.

"You said Haggard wants the bird. I think you meant the pot."

"See? I told you these two capers are almost identical."

"Well, they are in one sense. Bogart didn't have the falcon to begin with, and I don't have the Tompiro."

"You'll have it in just a few days."

27

~

A cigarette in one hand. The other one rapping on my door. Her eyes peering in just above the gold-leaf letters of SPIRITS IN CLAY, which pegged her at about five-ten.

Tristan had installed a remotely operated lock after I'd experienced some security issues. I left the remote on the counter, walked to the door and cracked it open.

"You Hubert Schuze?"

"Yes."

She pushed at the door. Even though my foot was wedged against it, she managed to slide it back a few inches. She was scrawny but wide-shouldered with sun-bleached hair and a wide mouth with parched lips.

"I need to talk with you."

I pointed at the icon of a cigarette with a red line through it. "You'll have to put out the cigarette."

She stepped away from the door. "Then we can talk out here because I am not going to waste this smoke."

I stepped outside and the door clicked behind me.

"I want the thirty thousand dollars Carl Wilkes gave you," she said.

I fanned away the smoke her words carried. "Who are you?"

"I'm his wife, and that money is community property."

I remembered telling Susannah I wouldn't have cavorted with Carl's wife if he had one. In her unique style, she'd responded, "And especially if he *didn't* have one."

So he *did* have one. Now I felt bad about not inviting her into the shop. What's a little smoke in the air compared to losing a spouse?

"I'm sorry about your loss."

She waved it away with a brown-stained hand. "Don't be. I'm surprised someone didn't plug him years ago." She must have seen the look on my face because she added, "We haven't lived together for years. Don't get me wrong. I liked him well enough. Even after we were separated, if one of us got the urge, the other would usually oblige. But he dealt with lots of pot thieves who carried guns, so it didn't come as much of a surprise that one of them used theirs."

I shuddered.

"We were still legally married when he bit the dust. That thirty thousand he gave you is mine."

"He *offered* me thirty thousand if I could get him a certain kind of pot."

"A Tompiro," she said.

"Right. But I didn't get it, so he didn't give me anything."

"You're lying, but I don't blame you. I didn't expect you to just hand it over. So I'm prepared to make you an offer. If you want to be technical about it, only half that money is mine. So you give me fifteen and you can keep the other fifteen."

"I'm sorry, Mrs. Wilkes. I don't know what Carl may have told you, but he didn't give me any money."

"Yeah, and the collector told me she didn't give Carl fifty thousand, and I know she was lying too, because I saw a Tompiro pot there when I went to see her. I couldn't ask her to give me the money, because she'd already given it to Carl, but I was hoping she might know what Carl did with it. I'm his executor. It isn't in his bank account."

She hung her head and shook it slowly. Then she looked back up. "You wouldn't happen to know where it is, would you? If you could lead me to the fifty thousand the collector gave him, I might let you keep even more of the money Carl gave you."

I sighed. "Listen to me. I never got the pot. Carl never gave me the money. If the collector has a Tompiro pot, it's likely one she already had. She was probably telling you the truth that she didn't pay Carl fifty thousand—just like I'm telling you the truth that Carl didn't pay me thirty thousand."

She lit another cigarette. "Carl wasn't much of a husband. Gone most of the time even before we separated. Had lot of secrets. But he tried to be a good provider. He said once he sold the Tompiro, he'd pay off my medical bills. I've got emphysema. I can't work. I need that money, Mr. Schuze."

"I liked Carl, Mrs. Wilkes—"

"Call me Thelma." She smiled and her lips cracked. She extracted some lip balm from her purse.

"Call me Hubie. I didn't get anything from him, Thelma. But even so, I'd be willing to help you out because he was my partner in a way. But I'm broke myself. I was counting on that money to pay my *own* medical bills and my mortgage and lots of other things. I wish I could help you, but right now I can't even help myself."

She rubbed a second coat of balm on her lips and moved them around like she was silently practicing diction.

"I'm still not sure I believe you, but you seem like a nice person. Carl always spoke highly of you."

I didn't comment.

"Maybe you could talk to the collector," she suggested. "She didn't want to admit to me that Carl sold her that pot, but she might admit it to you."

"Why would she do that?"

"You're a dealer. She might want to be on your good side in case there are other pots she wants."

I shook my head. "First of all, the collector didn't get the pot from Carl. Carl didn't have a Tompiro. That's why he asked me to find one. There's no way Carl just stumbled across one in the past few days. They're very rare. I've had only one in my twenty years in the business."

And sold it just last year, I thought to myself. To an elegant lady of a certain age named Faye Po. Then I thought about how different that sale was from most of my transactions.

Layton Kent, prominent citizen and—despite that—my attorney, had arranged the sale. The two of us had gone to Ms. Po's home, he carrying a sales contract, me carrying the pot in a shiny red gift box purchased by Mrs. Kent for the occasion.

We had tea and strange cakes. We exchanged pleasantries. We signed the papers using a Visconti pen with an eighteen-karat-gold nib and a double reservoir filling system. I thought ink reservoirs had disappeared because of all the shirts they ruined. But I suppose the reservoir in a pen that costs more than the average American makes in a year does not leak.

Now I was standing on the sidewalk haggling over pots and money with a woman I'd never before met, not even sure if she was who she claimed to be.

"The collector's name wouldn't happen to be Faye Po, would it?"

"No."

Of course not. Those two worlds never meet.

"And don't ask me what her name is," Thelma added, "because I won't tell you."

I asked instead about services for Carl.

"He didn't want any service. He told me that when he thought the cancer was going to kill him. 'How about just a simple memorial?' I asked him. He said not even that, and he made me promise." She wiped a tear from her cheek. "I ought to give up these cigarettes. They gave me emphysema and the damn smoke gets in my eyes." She rubbed another tear away. "He was a tough old bird. Only thing he really liked was work."

"And pots."

"He hated pots."

"He did?"

"Yep. Said they'd ruined his work. Like I said, he loved work. Loved gettin' it done. He was happiest when he was part of a big job, a long canal or a big dam. The bigger the project, the more he liked it. Gave him a sense of accomplishment, I guess. When we were courting, he'd drive me to see some big concrete culvert he made. Not very romantic, but I liked that he wanted to share that stuff with me."

"How did pots ruin his work?"

"It wasn't the pots—it was ARPA. I guess you know all about that."

Too well, I thought.

"After ARPA became law, they had to hold up every project while a bunch of archaeologists turned over every rock to make sure there wasn't an artifact or bone that might be disturbed."

I told her I remembered Carl telling me when he was talking about dragline and bucket operations that "every third scoop had an artifact in it."

"Yeah. So after ARPA he decided to start selling the stuff. It was partly the money and partly just because he didn't like the guys he described as namby-pambies who worked with brushes instead of backhoes. He could be ornery."

"Probably why he beat melanoma."

"Didn't help him much in the end."

Another few tears wetted her parched cheeks.

"Why do you not want to tell me the collector's name?"

"I don't want you and her to work something out behind my back."

"What could we work out behind your back?"

"Maybe she and you together would figure out where Carl hid the fifty thousand and split it fifty-fifty. She gets half her money back, you get most of what Carl would've paid you, and I get left out in the cold. That's why I want to be there when you talk to her."

Using my most charming tone and my most winning smile, I said, "First you say I seem like a nice person, and now you say I'd leave you out in the cold."

She smiled again. Her lips seemed a bit more supple. I guess the balm was working. "It would have been her idea, not yours. But I'd still be out in the cold."

"You're not a very trusting person, are you, Thelma?"

"You're married to someone like Carl who never shares information, you get a little suspicious, I guess."

She was weathered. Wore a simple cotton dress and running shoes. No jewelry or makeup. A no-nonsense look.

"I'm sorry," I said. "There's nothing I can do for you."

She ground out a cigarette on the sidewalk. "I need that money," she said. "I'll come back if I think of something else."

I watched her walk away, her wide shoulders slumping.

I turned to the door and tried the knob. I had locked myself out. I took that as an omen and headed over to Dos Hermanas.

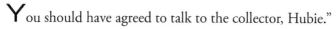

28

"You should have agreed to talk to the collector, Hubie."

"She wouldn't tell me who it is, so the only way I can do that is go with her."

"So? Why not go with her and at least find out who it is? Now that Carl isn't in the deal as middleman, you can get the whole fifty thousand if you sell the pot to the collector."

"I don't have the pot, remember? And the collector already has one. Maybe Thelma's right and Carl somehow found another Tompiro and sold it to the collector."

"Let's give him a name."

"Give who a name?"

"The collector. Aren't you tired of calling him that? Let's call him Reginald."

"Why Reginald?"

"Because rich people don't have names like Hank or Pete. They have names like Thurston or Reginald."

"Okay, but it can't be Reginald. The collector is a woman."

"So we'll make it Regina."

She pronounced it *reh-GEE-nah*, which is how we normally

hear it in the United States. But Sharice would pronounce it *reh-JI-nah* because that's how they pronounce the name of the capital city of Saskatchewan.

I saw no reason to argue the point. "Okay. But until I have the pot in hand, there's no reason to talk to her."

"You'll have the pot day after tomorrow."

"I wish you'd stop saying that. You're going to *cho bun* us."

"What's that mean?"

"It's a phrase I learned from Faye Po, the lady who bought the last Tompiro from me. It's when you start making plans for something good that you think is going to happen, but it doesn't happen because you took it for granted and started planning as if it were a done deal."

"Well, everyone knows about that special sort of jinx, Hubie. You don't need a Chinese word for it."

"Sure you do. There's no English word for it."

I signaled Angie while Susannah thought about it.

After Angie brought more salsa, Susannah asked if I'd finished my copy of the Tompiro pot.

I nodded and sat there staring into my margarita and thinking. "Thelma said Faye Po is not the collector, but I wonder if there's any connection between her and Regina."

"Wow. I hadn't even thought about that. In the Bernie Rhodenbarr murder with Rudyard Kipling, he steals a book from a collector, and the person who asks him to steal it is the person who sold it to the collector in the first place."

When Susannah gets excited about what might be a real-life murder mystery, she often tries to pack too many thoughts into one sentence.

"Rudyard Kipling steals a book?"

"No, of course not. Bernie steals the book. He's a burglar, remember?"

"Is the collector he stole it from named Regina?" I was trying to find the connection.

"No, he was named Jesse Arkwright. He bought the only copy of *The Deliverance of Fort Bucklow* by Rudyard Kipling."

"The other copies were by someone else?"

"How did you know there were other copies?"

"A lucky guess?"

"It seemed there was only one copy to begin with and a man named J. Rudyard Whelkin had it."

"There were two Rudyards?"

"Three if you count the lake."

I felt like I was losing the thread. "The lake?"

"Yeah, there's a Rudyard Lake in England. Whelkin," she continued, "sold the book to Arkwright, who paid a lot for it because he thought it was the only copy."

"Or at least the only copy by Kipling," I added.

She frowned. "Who else would write a copy of the same book?"

"Who else, indeed," I said, trying be amicable in the midst of my confusion.

"So Whelkin hires Bernie to steal the book back. And you already know why because you guessed there were other copies."

I did?

"Right," I said, "but remind me why there being multiple copies made Whelkin want to get the book back."

"Because he had another buyer who was willing to pay even more than Jesse Arkwright, but only because the new buyer *also* thought it was the only copy in existence. Whelkin discovered that Arkwright was going to advertise his copy for sale. If the new buyer saw that ad, he would realize the book he was about to buy was not unique and there might be any number of them floating around."

"Okay, but what does this have to do with the Tompiro?"

"It's obvious, Hubie. Regina has what she thought was the only Tompiro pot in existence. Then Carl offers to get her a second one. So Regina realizes her pot isn't as valuable as she thinks it is. She agrees to buy the pot from Carl. Except when Carl shows up, she kills him and destroys the other pot to make sure she still has a one of a kind."

"You're forgetting one small detail—Carl didn't have a Tompiro."

"He could have found another one. Maybe it was cheaper than the thirty thou you wanted for yours, so he bought that one instead."

"There is no way he found another Tompiro."

"You found one at White Sands on your first try."

"Only because I was able to search in a site no one has searched because it's inside the missile range. I scoured outside of the range on the east side of the Manzano Mountains for years and only found one intact pot."

"And it was on my family's land. You should pay me something for it."

"You were about eight years old when I found it. I'll give you a kid's portion."

"I'm just kidding. But Carl could have found another one."

"It's possible. There are a few in museums. There are more with cracks, chips and holes. And there may be some other intact ones to be dug up. But the odds that Carl found one are very long."

"So if Regina didn't kill Carl, who did?"

"Thelma," I said, because it's easier to indulge Susannah's murder mystery interest than to talk sense to her when she slips into her Nancy Drew persona.

"Why would Thelma kill him? She told you he was a good provider even after they separated. She doesn't work, so why cut off her money supply?"

"Maybe she wanted the whole fifty thousand."

"But she asked you to help her find it."

"Just a clever play to throw suspicion away from herself."

Her eyes narrowed. "You're just humoring me, aren't you?"

"Busted. I have no idea who killed Carl. Whit is investigating it. He doesn't need my help."

"You don't know if he needs your help or not. You may have a clue he doesn't know about."

"I don't have a clue."

"You said it. He was your partner, Hubert, and you aren't lifting a finger to bring his killer to justice."

"I told Whit everything I know. What else can I do?"

"Cozy up to Thelma. She might divulge something in an intimate moment."

"There is no way . . . you're kidding, right?"

"Two can play at that game."

We laughed and signaled for Angie. The timing was perfect because Sharice showed up just then to put in her order—a glass of Gruet.

I introduced Sharice and Susannah and each woman told the other the wonderful things I had said about her. When the drinks arrived, Susannah offered a toast to Sharice and me.

It was followed by an awkward silence.

29

I can't believe you invited her to join us without telling me."

"You don't complain when Martin or Tristan drop in on our cocktail hour unannounced."

I had just picked Susannah up for our trip to the Inchaustigui Ranch. It's closer to the missile range. The next day promised to be long and tiring. Starting from the ranch would make it a bit easier.

"I already know them, Hubert. It's different when it's somebody new. You should have told me."

"Why?"

"So I could prepare."

"Oh, come on. Sharice is not the Queen of England. You don't need to practice up on your curtsy before meeting her."

"You are so clueless. Have you ever heard the phrase 'You only get one chance to make a first impression'?"

"Yeah, and I've always wondered why people say it as if it's some nugget of wisdom. It's nothing but a tautology. You only get to do the first *anything* once—that's what *first* means."

"It *is* a nugget of wisdom. You just don't see that because as usual you're intellectualizing it. Labeling it as a tautology, whatever the hell that is. If you tried to understand the feeling part, you wouldn't sound so cold and clueless."

"Sorry," I said in my little-boy voice.

After a few seconds she exhaled audibly and said, "No, I'm the one who should apologize. I felt uncomfortable when she showed up. She's so elegant and so thin. I felt clunky."

"I—"

"Don't say anything. I'm happy for you, Hubie. She's not only strikingly beautiful, she's intelligent and articulate. And it's obvious from the way she looks at you that she's madly in love with you. You deserve that. Your love life hasn't been as rocky as mine, but no one would call it normal." She paused for a deep breath. "I didn't snap at you because I was unhappy with you as much as because I'm unhappy with myself. I don't know how she makes herself up and still looks so natural. I don't know how she walks without rocking like she's on a horse. I envy how she's thin without being skinny, how her long legs seem to go all the way up to her armpits. And most of all—God, this really hurts—I know I'll never be able to wear the fabulous clothes she wears because I'm too damned fat."

"Oh for heaven's sake. You are not fat. You're—"

"Watch it, Hubert. Dragging out the wrong euphemism could be dangerous."

I raced through the options, rejecting full-figured, buxom, statuesque and voluptuous. "Shapely," I said.

"At least you didn't say *full-figured*. I hate that."

Whew.

"Put little fairy wings on her," she said, relaxing a bit, "and she could be the black Tinker Bell. Designers would love her."

I decided not to comment.

We were on I-40 driving east through Tijeras Canyon, an apt name for the scissorlike pass between Albuquerque and the plains of eastern New Mexico.

I dislike freeways. I was looking forward to State Highway 14, where we could turn south onto a road with a view I could enjoy because the sun wouldn't be in my eyes and the semis wouldn't be on my tail.

I started laughing.

"What's so funny?"

"Women. I don't understand them."

"Well, boo-freakin-hoo. Of course you don't understand women. You're a man."

"I understand one thing about women."

"Yeah? What?"

"If Carl and I had been women, I would have known all about his family. I would have known he was married. I would have known whether he had children, which I didn't even think to ask Thelma about. I would have known whether he had sisters or brothers and I would have known all their names."

"So what did you two men talk about?"

"Work. Money. Pots."

"That's sad."

"It wasn't sad. We enjoyed talking to each other. But now that he's dead, I wish I had talked to him about more personal things. It just didn't occur to me. Anyway, I was going to tell you something about Sharice. After we got back to my place last night, she told me she felt intimidated in your presence. You're so curvy, and she saw the way all the guys were sneaking peeks at you."

"See why you should have told me? Knowing that she . . . well, I would have worn a loose-fitting blouse or something."

"She's not self-conscious about it, Suze. She mentioned it because she noticed the other guys, not because she's jealous. And she liked how you seemed self-assured in the bar and wished she could be like that. But she doesn't want big breasts. She knows she has that gamine look."

"You think my boobs are too big?"

"We're friends, Suze. I don't think about you that way."

"Give me a yes or a no."

"No. They aren't too big. And yes, even though we're friends, I do notice them. Happy?"

"Yeah."

"Good. Can we talk about something else?"

"Yeah. How about we go swimming in the stock tank when we get to the ranch? I have this skimpy bikini I'd like you to see." She started laughing. "That morning sun is powerful. We've only been on the road ten minutes and you're already glowing red."

"Very funny."

"You didn't answer me—do you want me to put on that bikini?"

"I'll bet you don't own a bikini."

"You're right. But it's fun to see you blushing."

We reached Highway 14. Not a minute too soon.

"Why are you turning here?" she asked. "Going through Moriarty is faster."

"This way is more scenic."

"And?"

I knew she had it figured out. "It takes us by some of the Tompiro sites."

After Escabosa and Chilili, we stopped at the Quarai ruins, a place so quiet and lonely it's hard to believe it's on the same planet as Albuquerque, much less an easy commute. The suburbs will reach out here soon. We destroyed a civilization. You'd think maybe we could at least let their spirits rest in peace.

Susannah pulled a brochure from the box next to the parking area and read it. "'The Franciscans taught the Indians the Spanish language, new agricultural methods and crafts.'"

"Crafts? Maybe like making wooden crosses during the winter, when many of the Indians froze to death for lack of firewood."

"The Indians aren't the only people who've been mistreated. My grandfather was eighteen when he got here. A guy met him at the railhead. He took him up into the Manzanos and gave him a tarp, bedroll, beans, bacon, cast-iron pot, rifle and canteen. Then he just left him there. At least there was a dog there. He knew a hell of a lot more about shepherding than my grandfather did."

"I thought Basques were natural shepherds."

"That's racial profiling, Hubie."

After we laughed, she continued her story. "He was actually a cook by profession."

"I figured since his name was Gutxiarkaitz he'd be a sleazy politician."

"I'm impressed that you remembered his name, but why would you figure him for a sleazy politician?"

"Because you told me Gutxiarkaitz means 'little rock,' which is the home of Bill Clinton and Mike Huckabee."

"Groan. Anyway, he contracted a bad case of *txamisuek jota*."

"That's like Lyme disease, right? Except carried by sheep instead of deer."

"Literally it means 'struck by sagebrush,' but what it actually means is depression."

"How did he get over it?"

"After he'd been there for several weeks, two cowboys showed up yelling at him. They were probably telling him to keep his sheep away from the land where they were grazing cattle, but he didn't speak English, so he just ignored them."

"Probably the wise course."

"Nope. They got his attention by trying to run him down with their ponies."

"Obviously, he survived."

"Yeah. He had quick reflexes because he was a champion at *zesta-punta*."

"*Zesta-punta?*"

"You know it as jai alai. As the first cowboy reached him, Aitona grabbed a stirrup, and in one fluid motion flung himself up to the saddle while pushing the cowboy to the ground. Then he turned the pony and lassoed the second cowboy. A few hours later, he rode into the cowboys' camp astride one horse with the second one tethered behind and the two cowboys tied across the saddle like bedrolls. The herd owner was so impressed he hired Aitona on the spot. After he learned English, he eventually became the head wrangler, and he ultimately ended up owning the acreage when the state put it up for sale."

I already knew that *aitona* means grandfather. I also knew her father's name is Eguzki, which means *sun* in Basque, but he goes by Gus. And her mother's name is Hilargi, which means *moon*, but she goes by Hilary.

They call Susannah *Sorne*, which means *conception* in Basque.

Susannah's voice pulled me out of my musings about her family. "You ever dig anything up here?"

"Never tried. Been picked over by too many archaeologists."

We leaned against the ancient walls, smelled the salt in the dry air and listened to the wind sing between the stacked rocks.

"Your parents know you're dating Baltazar?"

"Yeah, but they haven't met him. We aren't serious enough for that. Yet."

"And besides," I chided, "he never leaves La Reina."

"He's come to see me in Albuquerque twice."

"Must be true love," I said, and she took a swipe at me.

30

～

We climbed into the Bronco and headed south toward the Inchaustigui Ranch. I'd been nervous about the trip because the Inchaustiguis seem to be under the impression that Susannah and I are an item.

It created some awkward moments, which I handled poorly, largely because I didn't set them straight. I thought doing so would be stepping on Susannah's toes. She thought I had simply misinterpreted the situation.

Which is why I asked her about Baltazar. Since they knew she was dating Baltazar, I no longer had to worry about them thinking she was dating me.

The Inchaustigui home is an inviting two-story fieldstone structure surrounded by western catalpas and big reddish dogs with pointy snouts and floppy ears. They guard the place by charging at you like rockets and threatening to lick you to death.

After surviving the *Euskal artzain txakurra*—Basque sheep-dogs—I received a hug from Hilary and three crushing hand-shakes and rib-rattling slaps on the back from Gus and Susannah's two younger brothers, Matt and Mark.

We were seated at the long table in front of the fireplace drinking lemonade when Hilary said, "It's nice you two are marching to honor the memory of those poor boys. I cry every time I read about it."

All the New Mexico papers give it full coverage because almost 2,000 soldiers from the New Mexico National Guard were deployed to the Philippines in World War II and ended up in the Bataan Death March. Only half survived, and half of those died not long after the war because they were in such wretched condition.

After the Americans and their Filipino allies surrendered, 400 Filipino officers were summarily executed. The surviving Filipino and American soldiers were marched through the jungle with no food or water for the first three days of the trip. Those who fell or lagged behind were bayoneted. Some were beheaded by Japanese officers practicing with their samurai swords.

After the first three days, the prisoners were finally allowed water, but only from filthy water-buffalo wallows, which resulted in dysentery, worsened by the fact that the guards would not allow bathroom breaks. The prisoners had to foul themselves as they walked. The trucks carrying the Japanese guards drove over fallen prisoners.

Prime Minister Hideki Tōjō and Generals Masaharu Homma, Kenji Doihara, Seishirō Itagaki, Heitarō Kimura, Iwane Matsui, Akira Mutō and Baron Kōki Hirota were found guilty of war crimes and executed. They deserved worse. But it doesn't matter. Nothing can change what they did.

There are only fifty survivors of the Bataan Death March. More than half of them live in New Mexico.

The more Susannah and her family talked about the march in honor of these men, the guiltier I felt. I wasn't marching to honor them. I was marching to steal a pot.

And now it seemed to me that I wouldn't be marching. I'd be skulking.

I was trying to figure out some way to rationalize it when Hilary asked me how my pot hunting was going—not exactly a topic I was eager to discuss.

So I shifted the topic in her direction. "We stopped at Quarai on the way here, and that reminded me that I once dug up a Tompiro pot on your land. Of course, I didn't know you then. I sold that pot last year, and I told Susannah the other day that I should probably pay you for it."

Hilary laughed. "Having you with Sorne is payment enough. We always worry about her in the big city, but we feel a lot better because of you."

"Thanks," I said, hoping my discomfort wasn't too obvious as I wondered what "with Sorne" meant.

Matt rose and said to me, "Why don't you show Mark and me where you found that pot."

Matt drove his crew-cab pickup along a gravel ranch road for a few miles and then turned off toward Jumanes Knob. As he got closer, I gave directions that got us as near as a vehicle could take us. We walked a hundred yards, then climbed up a gentle slope, went behind an outcrop and then up a steeper slope that required holding on to roots exposed by erosion. A small cave was hidden by the top of the outcrop.

"Dad showed us this place when we were kids," Mark said. "I'm not sure I could have found it though."

Matt nodded. "You remember what he told us?"

"Some of it. I think I was about six."

"You were seven. I was nine. He held up an arrowhead: 'Other people lived here many years before we did. They made arrows to hunt buffalo, deer and antelope.' He picked up a shard. 'They made pots. They're broken now, but they used them for water.'"

"I remember asking for an arrowhead," Mark said.

"Yeah. Dad told us we could each pick out one we liked. We made a contest out of it, seeing who could find the best one."

"I think I did and you took it away from me."

"Sure. I was older. But you found another good one. Then Dad said, 'Those are gifts from the people who made them. But you have to leave all their other things alone.' 'But it's on our land,' I said. 'No,' he said, 'the land did not belong to them, and it doesn't belong to us. We are just the caretakers.'"

After a moment, Matt smiled and said, "Too bad Dad said that. We might have dug up that pot Hubie found and made a pile of money."

I looked at the mesa above us. "That wind farm wasn't up there when I was searching for pots. It was like I had the whole place to myself. I slept in a tent for three days."

"Wind farm," said Matt. "Strange term. They don't farm the wind, they just gather it."

"The first people here gathered," I observed. "It was salt. Then there was true farming—pinto beans. Now we've gone back to gathering."

Judging from the looks they gave me, my anthropological insight did not impress them.

Matt's expression grew serious. "Me and Mark talked this over. We think Susannah is just going through a period of uncertainty."

"Yeah," Mark chimed in. "Like when I decided to buy the diesel truck instead of the gasoline model. I was almost to the dealership in Albuquerque when I started wondering if I was about to make a mistake. I loved that diesel, but once you buy it, you can't just turn it back in. So I started having second thoughts. It was just fear of taking that final step, writing that check."

"You comparing our sister to a diesel truck?"

"No, I'm just saying that anyone can have a bit of doubt before taking a big step."

It was about here in the conversation that I realized the topic was me and my relationship with Susannah.

"We like you, Hubie," said Matt. "You're a stand-up guy. Solid. Got a good business. Mom and Dad like you too. This thing with Baltazar will blow over. We hope you won't bolt."

I'd let this confusion continue too long. It was time to be the stand-up guy they thought I was. I gathered up the courage to look Matt in the eyes and said, "Actually, I'm dating someone."

They both smiled. "See what we mean about you, Hubie? Straight shooting. That's what we value out here. Of course we know about Sharice. Susannah told us about her. When Susannah was describing her over the phone the other night, you could hear the jealousy in her voice. Your strategy is brilliant."

"My strategy?"

"We figured it out. Susannah starts dating a guy who's a bit different, a Hispanic guy who lives in a weird village—no disrespect to the guy or the village. So what do you do—mope around by your lonesome? Nosirree. You start dating someone even *more* exotic, a black beauty from Canada of all places. Brilliant. Absolutely brilliant."

I opened my mouth, but my brain passed on the opportunity to supply some words. The Inchaustiguis are a terrific family. It wasn't my place to break the news that Susannah and I are not romantically involved and never have been. That should be Susannah's job. My job is to convince Susannah that she needs to do it.

31

~

You must have misunderstood, Hubie. When Matt said your dating Sharice was a strategy, he meant a strategy for getting me away from Baltazar, not a strategy to win me over. I should have expected it. They were noticeably cool when I told them about Baltazar."

"What about when Matt said you're 'going through a period of uncertainty'?"

"That's true. I'm uncertain about how I want things to go with Baltazar."

"What about when they said, 'We hope you won't bolt'?"

"It's natural they'd want my best friend to stand with me during a period of indecision in my life."

This wasn't going the way I'd hoped. "But they said that after you started dating Baltazar, they liked that I didn't just mope around. That I started dating Sharice."

"What's wrong with that? I mope around when you're dating someone and it cuts into our margarita time and conversation. Of course, that hasn't happened much until now."

"Thanks a lot."

I was failing once again to convince Susannah that she needed to disabuse her family of the idea that we're a couple. Maybe she was right. If they did think we're a couple, surely they would've brought it up to her, ask her if the two of us have wedding plans or something like that. But I still wondered why Susannah was so unwilling to even consider the idea that her family—or maybe just her brothers—might think we're a couple. And why my attempts to convince her they do are so feeble. Maybe it's just an uncomfortable topic for both of us, so we want to cut short any discussion of it.

So I did what I too often do when the going gets rough.

I gave up.

Dinner conversation at the Inchaustigui table had mercifully stayed away from the topic of who was dating whom and why. So I had waited until the next morning when we were on the road to White Sands.

After I dropped the subject of Matt and Mark thinking Susannah and I are a couple, I asked her what Professor Casgrail said about the canvas Baltazar had given her.

"She said I should take it to the museum in Santa Fe and have them judge whether it's an O'Keeffe."

"Sounds good to me."

"That's because you haven't heard the rest of it. She said I should be prepared to leave it with them if it's a genuine O'Keeffe."

"Think of all the money you'd be walking away with."

"No. I wouldn't be *selling* it to them. I'd be *giving* it to them."

"Why would you give it to them? Make them pay. As far as I'm concerned, archaeology museums are just—"

"Places where pots go to die."

I smiled. "You have all my lines memorized."

"And I'll add one of my own: art museums are places where paintings by women go to be explained by men."

"Yeah. I remember the big O'Keeffe exhibit you dragged me to. They were her paintings, but most of the wall text was about Stieglitz."

"They still make him out to be the one who created her."

"And they're supposed to be experts? Don't give that painting to them, Suze. I'm sure O'Keeffe would rather it be with you than in that museum."

"Like you're sure the ancient pottery women want you to dig up their work?"

"Exactly."

She smiled.

Ansel Adams said, "When Georgia O'Keeffe smiles, the entire earth cracks open." He would've said the same about Susannah if he had known her.

"I know the canvas is dirty and has a little tear in it, but if you cleaned it up and stretched in on a frame, it would look good enough to sell."

"The reason she says I have to give it away is not because it's torn and dirty. It's because I don't own it."

"Of course you own it. Baltazar gave it to you."

"Yes, but it wasn't his to give. He didn't own it."

"He found it in the woods."

"That doesn't make it his. O'Keeffe never sold that painting, so her estate owns it."

"That's ridiculous. She never even finished it. She probably didn't like the way it was going so she tossed it away."

She was shaking her head. "Artists don't throw away paintings that aren't going well. They just keep working on them. And if they *do* give up, they save the canvas and paint something different on it. That's how we get a pentimento."

I couldn't resist. "I thought pentimentos grew on bushes and were mixed with cheese after they're harvested."

"Sheesh. A pentimento is when part of a painting flakes off to reveal an older painting underneath. It's exciting for art historians to discover a painting under a painting. And sometimes it can even be a clue in a crime."

"Don't tell me—let me guess. Because before they had closed-circuit cameras in banks, they used to hire artists to paint pictures of people at the teller cages demanding that money be put in a bag?"

"Make fun if you want to, but there was a murder solved when an X-ray of a 1471 Flemish painting revealed a painted-over message."

"I don't think they had X-rays in 1471."

"The *painting* was from 1471, Hubert. The X-ray was done just a few years ago by a woman named Julia, who was restoring the picture for a client who wanted to sell it."

"How did the painted-over message solve a murder?"

"The message under the paint was *Quis Necavit Equitem*." She turned to look at me, excitement in her eyes. "You can help me because you know Latin. I know the phrase means 'who killed the knight,' and I figure *Quis* must mean *who*. But which word is *knight*?"

"Good question. Technically the word *knight* is not in there. *Equitem* comes from *equus*—horse. So it refers to someone who owns a horse, hence, a knight. *Equitem* is the accusative."

"Why accuse the knight? He was the one who was killed."

I decided letting her get on with the story was better than explaining Latin declensions. "So whodunit?"

"I don't remember who killed the knight, but I know who killed Julia's friends."

"Huh? I thought Julia was the contemporary person restoring the painting. Why should her friends have anything to do with the killing of a knight in the fifteenth century?"

"It's all part of the chess game. This is perfect for you—chess and Latin."

I was beginning to feel lightheaded. "A chess match?"

"Yes. The painting depicts a nobleman and a knight playing chess while a young woman watches. The floor of the room they're in is tiled in black and white like a chessboard. So in addition to the arrangement of the pieces on the actual chess board, the three people in the painting are located on a floor that can also be seen as a chess board."

"That's ingenious."

"I figured you'd like it. But I had a hard time following the story because some of it depended on knowing that a chess piece in a certain location has a meaning. Like the woman being on a certain square indicating she was in danger of being checkmated."

"Women can't be checkmated. Only the king can be checkmated."

"See? I told you I didn't get it. The notes had abbreviations like Bc4 and Qd8-g5."

"What notes?"

"The notes from the killer."

"There were notes from 1471? What were they written on—parchment?"

"No, no. I'm talking about the contemporary murders. Julia asked her friends to help her figure out who killed the knight, and after they helped her, they were murdered. Someone didn't want the killer of the knight to be revealed."

"After five hundred years?"

"That seemed odd to me too. The murderer of her friends sent her notes with chess positions on them. So she got a local chess genius to help her figure out who killed the knight and who killed her friends. Can you guess the surprise ending?"

"Not in five hundred years."

"Come on. Give it a try."

"Okay. I'm going to guess that the person who killed the knight in 1471 also killed Julia's friends by biting them in the neck. Which explains how he lived so long—he was a vampire."

"Try to be serious."

"How can I be serious about such a bizarre story? I know evil geniuses are supposed to send notes to torment the incompetent police who are tracking them, but that only happens in fiction."

"This *is* fiction. *The Flanders Panel* is a murder mystery by Arturo Pérez-Reverte. It's a great book."

"But you said it was hard to follow."

"That's why they call them mysteries, Hubie. The murderer was someone who was always around when Julia and the chess expert were discussing the notes and trying to make sense of them. That was the surprise part."

"I think my vampire twist would've been a better surprise."

"Admit it. You initially thought I was talking about a real-life murder, didn't you?"

"You know what they say—truth is stranger than fiction."

"*They* say that, but you never do. If you read murder mysteries, you might be able to figure out who killed Carl."

"You read them. Maybe you can figure it out."

"Okay. It's almost always love or money. Maybe Thelma killed him."

"They've been separated for years. I don't think there's anything between them at this point that would cause a crime of passion."

"What about one of those times she told you about when one of them got the urge? Maybe she found Carl satisfying the urge with another woman."

"And killed her meal ticket?"

"That's why they call it a crime of passion. You're not thinking about your next meal when you pull the trigger."

I just shook my head. "You'd have to meet her. She's not the murderous sort."

"Then it's money. Regina killed him."

"Who is Regina?"

"The collector."

"Oh, right. I admit that's a possibility."

"Or Jack Haggard."

"Just because he had a card from a bail bondsman?"

"That and they were *associates*. A quarrel between partners in crime often leads to murder."

I admitted that was a possibility, although I didn't go along with her suggestion that Dotty and Donald were suspects, because I had no idea where they fitted in. Or *if* they did.

32

⁓

We continued kicking it around as we parked the Bronco and walked to the check-in table lit by generator-powered floodlights because it was still dark.

The MP—not either of the ones we encountered during our first visit—checked our IDs against the list of registrants and then looked through our backpacks.

He lofted the faux Tompiro I'd made so as not to arouse suspicion when I departed with the real one. No one would notice it wasn't the same pot.

"Why are you bringing a clay pot?"

"My energy bars are in it."

"Most people use Ziploc bags."

"It's my good-luck charm. I've never walked twenty-six miles before. I figure I need all the help I can get."

He dumped out the granola bars—homemade by Sharice with pearled barley, pomegranate syrup, sesame seeds and coconut flakes.

Yeah, that's what I thought too, before I tasted them.

He peered into the empty pot, put the bars back in it, handed it to me and said, "Whatever."

Susannah was right about the twenty-sixers being hardcore, especially the ones at the front of the throng. I speculated that the officials were placing people based on how they finished in the New York Marathon or their metabolism rate or body mass index or something. I didn't care because I didn't want to be near the front.

When the starting gun was fired, hundreds of people with not enough sense to be at home and asleep sprinted away. Those boxed in behind jogged on the heels of those ahead, biding their time until a lane for passing opened up.

Thirty minutes later, Susannah and I had managed to fall far enough behind the twenty-sixers that they wouldn't notice us if we left the trail. Which would have been true even had we been only a single stride behind, because no one was looking back.

We were not far in front of the leaders of the fourteeners. They could see us clearly if we left the trail. But when we rounded the next curve, they couldn't and we did.

Or rather I did. Susannah stayed by the side of the trail to make sure no one saw me and—if they did—to warn me with a whistle if they decided to head in my direction. After a couple of minutes, I was out of earshot, so she no longer had to worry about whistling and could read the Bernie Rhodenbarr book she brought along. At least she could when it got lighter out.

It would've been perfect had the arroyo I scooted into been the one where I buried the Tompiro. But real life is seldom perfect.

The topo map had the triangulation marks I'd made when I buried the pot. The sun was still below the horizon, but there was enough light to see the profiles of the peaks. One look at the compass told me I was too far south. How far south I didn't know. I was using a handheld compass, not professional surveying tools.

I walked north, checking the angle every five hundred yards or so. When it appeared I was close to the correct angle, I began checking the hill to the west. The closer I got, the slower I went because I had to check more often, and I had to check all three points. I'd just checked the two peaks for about the twentieth time and turned to the hill. I cradled the compass in my hand and looked up to locate the peak just as the sun rose over the Oscura Mountains.

Those two famous musical notes—*ta* and *da*—played in my head. I was standing next to the dune where I buried the pot. Sometimes real life is perfect. I pulled the fake out of my backpack in preparation for making the exchange.

An hour and a half later, I found Susannah where I'd left her. There were still people scattered along the route as far as I could see in both directions, but they were in small clumps or alone. Some were the stragglers of the fourteeners, some were the twenty-sixers making their second pass at that part of the trail, and some were probably just lost.

A few people were within earshot, so I didn't say anything. I took the pot out of my pack, held it in my hand and started walking.

Susannah fell in next to me and said, sotto voce, "Wow, I knew you were good at copies, but this is beyond amazing. Even though you made it from memory, the real one looks *exactly* like your copy."

"There's a reason for that," I said, and heard the emotional pain in my voice. "This *is* the copy."

She stopped. "I thought the plan was to leave the fake here. How are you going to explain arriving with one pot and leaving with two?"

"I'm not leaving with two. This is the fake, and it's the only pot I have. The real one is gone."

"Gone?"

"Yeah. Gone. As in not there."

"Not there?"

"Right. As in dug up and carried away."

"You must have dug in the wrong place."

"Impossible. First, I had the triangulation points from our previous visit, and they all lined up. Second, I recognized the spot. And finally, my rebar was there. Someone stole the pot."

"Yeah—you."

I was too depressed to argue the pot-thief issue. "Someone stole it from the dune after I stole it from the cliff dwelling."

We were silent while an elderly couple passed us. They wore big floppy hats and matching T-shirts that read FIT AS A FIDDLE AND JUST AS STRINGY.

Susannah started walking again, so I trailed along beside her. After a few seconds she said, "Carl Wilkes."

"You think Carl followed us out here?"

"It would explain how the collector got the pot Thelma said she saw."

"Yeah, but—"

"And it would explain why Thelma was so sure Carl paid you for the pot. Because he had it. She just didn't realize he got it himself rather than from you."

"Okay, I agree it all fits. But somehow I can't see Carl double-crossing me like that."

"You've always refused to see his dark side."

"Thank you, Obi-Wan Kenobi."

"Did you tell Carl you were coming out here to look for the pot when they had the Trinity Site visitation event?"

"I did." I felt like an idiot.

"I think that cinches it. He came out here, went to the Trinity Site and hid out behind the crowd. He probably spotted me alone and knew that meant you were off looking for a pot. Remember I told you I was one of the last cars to leave, and I stopped and let people pass until there was no one behind me? One of those people who passed must have been Carl. He made a mental note of where I was. Then he came back and dug up the pot."

"How did he get back in?"

"He was in the Corps of Engineers. Maybe he has connections with someone at the range."

"I don't know, Suze. It all sounds so bizarre."

"You have another theory?"

"Maybe it was that MP. He also saw where we were stopped, and it would be easy for him to go back and dig up the pot since he lives right here on the range."

"And he would go back and dig around because . . . what? He figured anyone who pees on his pants is probably a pot thief?"

"It was water."

"So you claimed. But you have to agree there was no reason for him to think you'd buried a pot. Or anything else for that matter."

I nodded and we started walking again.

When I'd told Fletcher that Carl hadn't told me the name of the collector, he'd responded, "'Course not. Probably afraid you might cut out the middleman." Carl was the middleman at that point. As the first man, my job was to find a pot. As the third man—make that third woman—Regina's job was to buy the pot. And as the middleman, Carl's job was to make a bundle by moving the pot from me to Regina and making sure Regina and I never met.

But by stealing the pot from the dune, Carl had cut me out. And now he was dead. My first thought was there had to be a connection. My second thought was that my first thought was from hanging around so much with Susannah.

Then I remembered that when I told Whit to be careful because Regina might be the murderer, Whit said, "You'd make a lousy cop, Hubert. If the buyer was gonna kill Wilkes, he would've done it *after* he got the pot."

Actually, I didn't tell Whit that Regina might be the killer. I didn't even know her as Regina at that point.

But regardless of the name, it made sense that the collector did exactly what Whit said: killed Carl after he delivered the pot.

33

～

There were four MPs checking people on the way out, but the lines were short because most participants stayed for the closing ceremonies, during which awards and citations were given out for things like first place in the marathon, oldest participant, most years of consecutive attendance and so on.

There was no award for most disappointed participants, so we skipped the ceremony in order to get an early start back to Albuquerque.

I chose the line with the MP who had checked me in. He looked into my pot and said, "Your energy bars are still in there."

"That must explain how tired I feel."

He returned the pot and my other belongings.

Susannah drove the Bronco on the grounds I was so depressed I might run off the road.

It was past ten when I let myself into my residence. I placed the fake pot on the kitchen table. Geronimo was happy to see me. He must have sensed my mood because instead of begging for food, he plopped down at my feet and stared up at me with those sad eyes.

I opened the bottle of Gruet I'd planned to drink in celebration. I didn't feel like cooking, so I reached into the pot and pulled out one of Sharice's energy bars. It didn't energize me, but it went great with the champagne. I gave an energy bar to Geronimo. He liked it too. I filled his water bowl and my champagne flute. Even in the bottomless pit of depression, I don't drink Gruet from the bottle.

When the alcohol began to kick in, I stopped feeling sorry for myself and started wondering how I was going to avoid foreclosure. I reached for another energy bar, but the pot was empty.

The pot! That's it. Sell the fake. Pass it off as real and get $50,000. Like Susannah had said about *The Maltese Falcon*, although I couldn't remember exactly how that was similar.

I congratulated myself for having maintained my craftsmanship even when fabricating a fake I had planned to leave buried in the sand dune. The fake had returned home with me, the plan it was created for having been thwarted by the disappearance of the real pot it was supposed to replace. But the fake was good enough to pass off as the real thing to anyone except a trained expert. And while the buyer I had in mind probably knew more about pots than the average citizen, I didn't figure him for a true expert.

It's against my code of ethics to lie about a fake pot. If someone offers to buy one of my replicas at the price penned on the discreet little tented card in front of it, I see no reason to broach the issue of authenticity. If they ask me whether a pot is genuine, I say, "Of course."

Well, it's a genuine *pot*, isn't it?

But if they ask me whether it's old, I tell the truth.

Would Jack Haggard ask? I doubted it. He knew that Carl—his *associate*—had sent me on a mission to find a genuine Tompiro. If I placed the pot in front of him, he would assume I had succeeded.

34

I woke up in my chair. Never a good start to the day.

I glanced down without moving my head. An empty bottle of Gruet was on the floor next to Geronimo. He likes champagne, but my hangover told me he was not the one who had drained the bottle.

I nudged him with a foot. He opened one eye.

"Get me some coffee," I said.

"Arf," he replied. He stood up and walked over to a kitchen cabinet. It was not the one with the coffee. It was the one with the dog food.

There was a knock and then Glad's voice asking through the door if I was home. I told him to come in. When he did so, I asked him, without getting up or even turning my head, to make me some coffee and feed Geronimo. In that order.

"Had a bad night, did we?"

"After a bad day. Hope yours was better."

"It wasn't. I was almost struck whilst walking on the verge."

"On the verge of what?"

"I think you Yanks call it the shoulder. Strange phrase.

Anyway, a lorry almost struck me and didn't even stop to see if I was all right."

"If she didn't stop, how do you know she was a Laurie and not a Jane or a Mary?"

"Not Laurie—lorry, a truck."

"Ah."

While the coffee brewed, I told him about my second trip to the missile range and the pot being stolen.

"Must have been Wilkes," he said.

"That's what Susannah thinks."

"Aced her O-levels, I should think. I told you Carl was dodgy. So now what?"

"How about you pay me five years' worth of lease payments in advance?"

He laughed. "If I don't get the shop started soon, I'll be making the payments in arrears, if at all. Are things really so bad?"

I nodded. "I need money and I need it now. The problem is a high-end pot store is not like a pharmacy or gas station. I don't have a steady stream of income. It's either feast or famine."

"And you're currently in a famine."

"Of biblical proportions."

"All right then. Here's what you do. Have a markdown sale."

I probably wrinkled my nose. I don't like to sell my pots even at the inflated prices I have on the tented cards. The idea of marking them down like last fall's fashions is disgusting.

He evidently read my mind. "I know what you're thinking. Tiffany's doesn't mark down diamonds. But instead of *not* selling one pot for thirty thousand, how about *actually* selling two for fifteen thousand each?" He handed me a cup of coffee and opened a can of food for Geronimo.

He poured himself some coffee. "A big markdown. Just this one time. To meet an emergency."

When he put it like that, it was a bit less distasteful. "I'm not sure a markdown sale would work for me."

"Why not?"

"Well, suppose a basic BMW sells for fifty thousand. If I advertise I have them marked down to twenty-five thousand, people will line up to buy them. But selling pots is not like selling cars. There's no Blue Book for ancient Indian pottery. So if I say this pot, previously listed at thirty thousand, is now available for only fifteen, most people will just say it was overpriced at thirty and—who knows—maybe still is at fifteen."

"You won't know if you don't try."

His enthusiasm was bolstering. But I was still uncomfortable with selling any pot at a discount. I've spent most of my adult life collecting my inventory, fighting back acrophobia to climb into places I'd rather not be, digging holes with my bare hands, sleeping rough in the desert.

"I have another plan to get some money," I told him. "If it doesn't work, I'll consider your sale idea."

35

~

The pistol in Jack Haggard's hand confirmed my suspicion that calling him had been a bad idea.

The suspicion—based on nothing specific at first—had begun to form when he arrived wearing a jacket on a warm, sunny day.

At least he had the good sense to protect himself from UV damage with a broad-brimmed hat pulled down to ear level.

The pot was on the counter. He took off his hat so he could get his face close to it. He must have liked what he saw.

"What's the deal?" he asked.

"Same as what I agreed to with Carl—thirty thousand dollars."

"Okay. I'll give you a check."

The suspicion grew larger. Like all forms of commerce where a paper trail is unwanted, the illegal antiquities trade is cash only. And that's what I asked for.

"I'll have to bring it to you after the collector pays me," he said.

"I never let a pot leave the store until it's paid for in full."

And that's when he reached into the jacket and came out with the pistol.

"I'll make an exception in this case," I said.

He picked up the pot with his free hand. "Don't try anything stupid."

"No problem. I'll just wait here until you bring my share of the deal."

He smiled. "Yeah, you do that."

As soon as the door shut behind him, I ducked under the counter. I didn't think he was going to take a shot at me through the window, but why take a chance? And I knew he couldn't get back in because of Tristan's high-tech automatic lock.

I'll tell you, I felt a lot better cowered behind the counter than I had facing that pistol. I know nothing about guns. I don't know if it was a .357 or an eight and a half. All I know is it was pointed at me.

I was still sitting below the counter when Whit Fletcher responded to my call. I peeked around the corner, then hit the remote and stood as he entered.

Whit made second team All State as a defensive tackle at Tucumcari High School back in the '70s. He's a bit over his playing weight these days, but he carries it well. His hair is silver and usually in need of a trim, and his eyes slant down like he's either part Asian or in need of a nap. But there's something about his cop demeanor and steady gaze that inspires confidence.

"I've been robbed."

"I'll call someone from robbery detail."

"I think you'll want to handle this one yourself. Remember that pot Carl Wilkes wanted me to find?"

"Yeah, the tom-tom. I don't usually forget something worth fifty thousand."

"Tompiro."

"Whatever. That what the robber took?"

Well, you know what Haggard took was a fake. But if I told Whit that, he'd want to know how I copied something I don't have. Then I'd have to explain that I'd seen the real one but couldn't get it off the range the first time and discovered it had been stolen when I returned. So I just kept it simple.

"Yeah. And he's going to sell it to the collector Carl was dealing with."

"How do you know that?"

"The guy who robbed me is named Jack Haggard. He came here a few days ago and said he was working on a deal with Carl. He asked about the Tompiro. I didn't have the pot, but I didn't tell him that. In fact, I didn't tell him anything. But then I got a pot and called him. When he came in, he said he would bring the cash after he sold the pot. I told him my policy is never to let a pot leave the shop until the cash is in my hands."

"And he changed your policy with a Smith and Wesson."

"I don't know what brand of gun it was."

"It's just an expression. You got a plan in mind?"

"When you locate him, maybe you shouldn't arrest him. Just have him tailed until he sells the pot. Arrest him during the transaction. I know criminals can't keep money they get illegally, so maybe you could confiscate the fifty thousand he gets from the collector."

"It ain't quite that simple. More than likely the collector is gonna give him a check. Unlike you pot thieves, most people don't like to deal in cash. And even if he does pay in cash, it goes into a special safe. We don't keep cash in the evidence locker."

"So I guess there's no way we can split the fifty thousand."

"I didn't say that. I just said it ain't gonna be easy."

"You know who Regina is?"

"She got a last name?"

"Sorry. What I meant to say is do you know who the collector is?"

He gave me a weird look. "Not yet. Maybe we can work it from the seller's end rather than the buyer's. Gimme a description of Haggard."

"How about a picture instead?"

I opened the laptop Tristan set up for me. It's connected to a camera that takes a shot of the door every time it opens. I selected the third item back on the list because the first one would be Fletcher entering and the second one would be Haggard leaving.

All we could see was the hat.

I gave Whit the card on which Haggard had written *tompiro* and then added his phone number.

Whit extracted his little notebook. "How tall was he?"

36

～

Y ou knew the guy had dealings with a bail bondsman. Why did you have the pot sitting on the counter like a grab-n-go sandwich?"

Susannah had pushed her margarita aside and was leaning forward slightly as she does when she's scolding me.

"I figured if he saw it the moment he came in, he'd think it was the pot I got for Carl and wouldn't ask any questions about it. That way I wouldn't have to lie about it being real."

"So you made it easy for him to steal the pot because even though you were going to swindle him, you didn't want to lie to him?"

"He probably deserves being lied to. But if I can break my rule based on who I'm talking to, it isn't much of a rule."

"Your ethics are weird, Hubie. Consistent, but weird. Why didn't you want to report it as a robbery?"

I dipped a chip into the salsa and ate it.

"Oh. You're hoping Whit can get the money instead of the pot."

I nodded as I washed the chip down with my margarita.

"Does he know who Regina is?"

"No. And I actually asked him if he had discovered who Regina is. I wish we hadn't started calling her that."

"Well, the woman waited a long time for that pot, Hubie. She deserves to have a name at least."

"Even if it isn't hers?"

"Sure. Maybe she doesn't like her current one—Hilda, Prudence, something like that."

"Well, we know as much about her location as we do her name."

"I thought Whit was going to find out who she is."

"He's trying, but they have nothing to go on. Carl didn't tell me her name of course, and he also didn't let any clue slip out. For all I know the woman lives in Katmandu."

"Katmandu! Yes. This *is* like the Rudyard Kipling story."

"'Rikki-Tikki-Tavi'?"

"No, *The Deliverance of Fort Bucklow*."

"I thought that was a forgery."

"Exactly."

"Huh?"

"After Bernie has stolen *The Deliverance of Fort Bucklow*, the wealthy maharajah who's after it sends his Sikh servant to the bookstore to steal it. He pulls a gun on Bernie just like Haggard pulled a gun on you. Bernie hands him a copy of a different Kipling book, and the Sikh doesn't know it's not *The Deliverance of Fort Bucklow*. So he takes it, just like Haggard took a pot from you without knowing it wasn't the real Tompiro. So even though he robbed you, you get the last laugh."

I took a deep breath. "In the first place, Katmandu is not in India, so I don't see the connection. In the second place, the maharajah will know it's the wrong book as soon as he sees it.

But Regina won't know the pot's a fake. So Haggard will get the fifty thousand even though it isn't a real Tompiro, and that makes me want to cry, not laugh."

She gave me a half grin. "Spoilsport."

37

I told Glad the next morning that we were going with his mark-down plan.

"The plan you mentioned fell through?"

"At gunpoint," I said.

He raised his eyebrows. "Again!"

"I told you about the other times?"

"Didn't you?"

I guessed I must have. I don't like to dwell on those events, so I plowed ahead. "I can't do this myself. I'm too attached to the pots. I want you to do it. I have a list of people who've expressed interest in particular pots but either didn't have enough to buy them or weren't quite willing to make the leap. Some of these people come by so frequently they're almost like friends. They check to see if the pot they want is still here. I'll call them and tell them about the sale."

"You should also post an advert outside."

There were only thirteen people on the list. Two of them told me they had bought a similar pot elsewhere, and I could tell from their tone that they felt guilty about it.

As well they should. They discovered the sort of pot they wanted at Spirits in Clay. They took a proprietary interest in it, dropping by periodically to make sure I still had it. They even asked me to notify them before I sold it so they'd have a chance to buy it. They drank my coffee. Then when I call them about the pot, they say they've bought one elsewhere.

They wanted me to call them before I sold, but did they call me before they bought? Would it have been too much for them to call and say, "Hi, Hubie. I've found one of those Mogollon pots at another shop. It's priced lower than yours. You've put up with me constantly dropping in to see that pot, so I thought I'd ask if you could mark it down to what this fellow wants for his because I'd rather buy from you."

I managed to reach only seven of the remaining eleven on the list. One said he was no longer interested at any price, four thanked me for the call but were noncommittal, and two said they would be in as soon as possible. I told them Glad would be minding the shop and they could deal with him.

My building has a sort of shadowbox on the east wall, a shallow three-feet-by-four-feet wooden frame with a glass front and a hinged top. I assume it was built to hold adverts, as Glad calls them. I never use it. The merchandise is clearly visible through the windows. If that doesn't draw them in, a few words on a sign are not going to do it. But I hand-lettered one announcing a sale and dropped it into the box. Probably a waste of the parchment paper I use for cooking.

A thought that made me hungry and therefore doubly happy that I'd arranged a brunch date with Sharice to keep me out of the shop. I walked to the Grove, a popular restaurant in EDo (east downtown).

I suspect this acronymic naming craze started in New York with SoHo—South of Houston. Now there's LoDo (lower downtown) in Denver, SoDo (south of the dome) in Seattle and EDo in Albuquerque. The trendy name for east downtown hasn't done much for the area. The building the Grove occupies is fine but across the street are a sandy vacant lot and a cheap motel with brackish water in the bottom of the abandoned pool.

Sharice's condo is only a few blocks from the Grove. She was waiting in line when I arrived. After we studied the menu, she settled on the organic egg-white frittata with arugula, pecorino cheese and seasonal vegetables. I don't know why they describe it that way—who would serve unseasonable vegetables?

I chose the croque madame—tomato, whole-grain mustard, Gruyère cheese and a sunny-side-up egg open face on rustic farm bread. In deference to Sharice, I had them hold the Black Forest ham.

They gave us our coffees and a little stanchion with our number on it. I had to balance the tray in my hands for only five minutes before a table came open. That's less time than it usually takes at the popular restaurant.

"It didn't bother you to order a woman's sandwich?" Sharice asked once we were seated.

"With you clinging to my arm, no one is going to question my manhood."

"You didn't have to make it meatless on my account."

"I know that. But when you cut the ham they give you a second egg."

"They never do that when I order it."

A young woman arrived with our tray and topped off our coffee. "There's an extra egg on there for you, sweetie," she said to me as she left.

"Sweetie? So it's just the handsome guys who get the extra

egg. I thought you might bring the pot to show me, but I guess it's too valuable to carry around?"

"It is. But the reason I didn't bring it is I don't have it."

I told her about the trip, including Susannah and Glad both immediately seizing on Carl as the thief. She agreed that made sense.

"I know digging up an old pot makes you feel like you've rescued it. And you think the potter who made it would be happy it's being enjoyed again."

"Not *would be* happy. *Is* happy."

"You think her spirit is around?"

"Maybe. Maybe it's tied to the pot somehow."

"We all leave things behind when we die, but I doubt we're tied to them."

"Would you like the idea of your wardrobe being on display in a clothing museum after you're gone?"

"I guess I would, actually, although I know that's irrational."

"Maybe not."

"Let's say that Carl did take it from that sand dune," she said. "Does the fact that he didn't care about the potters make you feel any different about the pot being dug up?"

"Yes. I'd try to find it a good home. Carl would sell it to someone who planned to grind it up if the money was right."

At the Grove, you pay when you order, so I left a tip and we headed out.

"Your place or mine?" she asked.

"Yours," I said. "It's closer and Glad is in mine."

As we walked west along Central, she reminded me that I made a pass at her the second time we met. I'd just had a root canal, which required a big dose of anesthetic. After Dr. Batres finished, Sharice let me gargle and spit—not a good opening for a pickup line. Then she removed my bib and wiped off my face.

"I asked you if I could have a drink after the anesthetic wore off."

"And I said, 'Sure.'"

"Then I said, 'How about sex?'"

She laughed. "I'd never had anyone ask that, but I knew the anesthetic has no effect after it's worn off, so I said, 'Sure.'"

"And I said—"

She recited my line. "'Great. What time do you get off work?' Could you tell I was flustered?"

"No. But I was happy you laughed. I was afraid you might be offended."

"I thought it was sweet. And it worked. You finally got me in bed."

"Yeah, five years later."

She grasped my hand. "We need to make up for lost time."

I stepped up our pace.

Savannah cats are highly intelligent. When Benz saw us enter the condo hand in hand, he walked over to the balcony door and waited for Sharice to open it.

38

We spent the next three hours in the condo.

Use your imagination.

We agreed to meet at Dos Hermanas. She wanted to freshen up. I walked to Old Town in a warm cloud of contentment and took Geronimo for a walk.

After two rounds of the Plaza, I sat down on the banquette in front of San Felipe de Neri Catholic Church, the spiritual heart of Albuquerque for more than three hundred years. A sign was posted outside:

> *Clases de Catecismo en Español—todas edades.*
> *Martes, 6:30pm–8:00pm, en el Salón Parroquial*
> *junto a la iglesia.*
> *Primer Grado–High School, incluyendo clases de*
> *preparación para la Primera Comunión.*

Typical of New Mexico, I reflected, that *High School* was written in English. There was no reason for it, just as there is no reason why Spanish words find their way into most conversations in English out here. We joke about Spanglish, but this is bilingualism at its best. English and Spanish don't compete. They just lazily intermingle as people use whatever word pops to mind.

"You are planning to attend the catechism classes, Youbird?"

The voice was unmistakable, a rumbling basso profundo with an Eastern European accent you could cut with a kielbasa. Father Groas is over six feet tall, tips the scales at close to an eighth of a ton and has a thick bushy beard.

"I'm a bit old for that, aren't I?"

"The sign says *todas edades*."

"Would it help me deal with being in love?"

He sat down beside me and patted Geronimo on the head. "So your relation with Miss Clarke grows serious?"

"You know about her?"

"Yass. Someone mention her to me. A friend who worry that you will have problems."

If, as I immediately assumed, the friend was Miss Gladys, I wasn't bothered that she mentioned it to Father Groas. In fact, I was happy she cared about me enough to do so. I suspect she never saw a black/white couple growing up in East Texas in the '40s.

She is flustered when we talk about it. Not because she's opposed to it but because she's so worried she might say the wrong thing, so she tiptoes around the topic.

She's not the only one. It seems to be a national obsession. Some official in our nation's capital was fired recently for using *niggardly*, a term derived from an Old Norse word that meant to worry about small things and thus came to mean *stingy* in English. It is not derived from the Latin word for black and has nothing to do with the N word. Yet you can now be fired not only for using the N word (which would be justified) but also for using a word that *sounds* like it.

What's next? Will we be unable to say someone has *pluck* because it sounds like the F word? Or *flitch* because it sounds like the B word? Or, if you say it the Canadian way, *Regina* because it sounds like the V word?

"What do you think, Father?"

"It doss not take great wisdom to know that a mixed couple will have some problems. But is not important. Marriage is a gift from God, who we are told in Genesis created us in His image as male and female. The sacrament of marriage makes of the husband and wife one flesh. So if you and Miss Clarke marry, you will not be different colors—you will be one flesh."

"But I will still be white and she will still be black."

"You must look beyond appearances, Youbird, and reach for the deeper truths."

It sounded like good advice.

"What about you, Father? Were you ever in love?"

His hand disappeared into his beard. I assume he was stroking his chin. Or looking for a lost button. Who knows what's in there?

"Yass. Was a teacher in my village. She was pearhaps not so good a teacher. She taught me English," he said, and shook as he laughed. "Bot she was beautiful, and I wish she was not married. And I thought it was because of her that I am not interested in the girls of the village. Bot was probably because I know that I am not handsome man, and they will not like me. Bot later I realize I want to serve all people, so I become a priest."

"The Church is lucky to have you."

39

~

I walked to my residence and let myself in through the back door in the alley. I called Susannah to inquire if she minded Sharice joining us for drinks, an afterthought since I had already invited her.

"You don't need to call me now. I already missed the chance to make the right first impression." I know her so well that the level voice didn't fool me. She was still a bit miffed.

"Well, despite my insensitivity, you made a great impression on her."

"If you say so. See you both when you get there."

I went through the workshop to the shop and invited Glad to the cocktail hour, figuring a fourth might help avoid any awkward moments.

Sharice arrived while I was doing so.

"You'll be buying," he said, and beamed, his face even pinker than usual.

"You made a sale?"

"The Anasazi with the crooked bottom and the small crack."

"Sounds like a girl I used to date," I said, and Sharice poked me in the arm.

Glad handed . . . no, that doesn't sound right. Glad *gave* me a check for $10,000 from the fellow who'd been admiring that pot for three years.

I felt more or less as I expected to. I was sorry to know I'd never again own that pot, maybe never even see it. And I was unhappy that it had sold for a third of what I was asking. I thought we had agreed on half off, not two-thirds off. But I didn't want to be niggardly. After all, I'd paid only $1,000 for it a few years back. So even if you factor in inflation, the return on investment was healthy. But most important, I needed the money. Better to pay the mortgage than to have the pot, I told myself.

My self replied that I was right.

So the bounce in my step as our threesome entered Dos Hermanas and joined Susannah at our table was not solely from the romantic day spent with Sharice.

Angie surveyed the group and said, "Two margaritas, one without salt, a glass of Gruet Blanc de Noir, and a pink gin."

I showed Susannah the check.

"Great. Even though you already said I won the bet, this cinches it."

"What was the wager?" asked Glad.

"I told Hubie that having you mind the shop in his absence would increase sales. He didn't think so because he claimed that people who want an expensive pot are not impulse buyers so it doesn't matter if he's not there—they'll just come back when he is."

"Maybe once or twice," said Sharice. "But then they might lose patience and buy something else."

Susannah said, "That's what I told him," and looked at Sharice with an expression of camaraderie.

"What would they buy instead?" I challenged. Although I was pleased that détente might settle on Sharice and Susannah, I wasn't willing to abandon my belief that pots are not just another high-end piece of merchandise competing with BMWs and Rolexes.

But Sharice had the perfect rejoinder.

"The pot I have was given to me," she said, sneaking a glance at me. "But if I'd gone to Spirits in Clay two or three times to buy it and the place was closed, I would have gone shopping for a Georgia O'Keeffe painting instead."

It isn't much of a coincidence that Sharice mentioned O'Keeffe. Everybody out here mentions her. She's as much a part of New Mexico as green chile. You can peg a New Mexican's economic status by whether they own an O'Keeffe painting or merely a print.

When I didn't reply, Susannah said, "She got you, Hubie. Even you would admit that some of your best customers might prefer an O'Keeffe to a Maria."

"Maybe. But if they can afford an O'Keeffe, they're rich enough to also buy a pot."

"Especially now that you're having a fire sale," she said, and I winced.

"When you said you were going for brunch, I didn't realize I'd be minding the shop so long," Glad said to me. "What were you two up to all afternoon?"

Sharice and I glanced at each other.

There was the predictable awkward silence.

Susannah laughed. "They probably won't want to answer that."

"I see," he said, a bit embarrassed but not enough to stop him from adding, "A bit of slap and tickle, I suppose."

"Hubie doesn't know what that means," Susannah said to no one in particular, "because he doesn't watch the BBC shows on PBS."

"And I don't watch PBS shows on BBC, but I think I can guess."

Glad said, "I hope I didn't offend you, Miss Clarke."

"Not at all. And please call me Sharice."

We left after two rounds and much banter and ran into Miss Gladys heading toward my shop with the dreaded gingham bag.

I thanked her for thinking of me but explained that Sharice was cooking for me.

"Oh, pshaw. I knew that as soon as I saw she was here. I brought this for Gladwyn."

Gladwyn? She always calls me Mr. Schuze.

"How very kind of you," Glad said. "And what delight have you brought?"

"New Mexican chop suey."

A muscle in my stomach quivered.

"Brilliant," he said, and—taking the bag from her—led her into his shop with his free hand on her elbow.

"I hope you can join us for dinner," Sharice said to Susannah after our companions had closed the door. "I can guarantee it won't be chop suey, New Mexican or otherwise."

Susannah was still staring at the door. "Gladwyn and Gladys. Why am I not surprised?" Then she looked at us as if she had just then heard the invite. "Thanks, Sharice, but there is no way I'm going to be a third. Maybe another time when the numbers are different. I do look forward to sampling your cooking. Hubie raves about it."

She kissed each of us on the cheek and left.

40

The next few days were a blissful interlude in my vexations. Of course, I didn't know that at the time because interludes require both a before and an after.

The *before* vexations were clear enough. I had failed on two attempts at the simple task of carrying a two-pound piece of clay out of the White Sands Missile Range, and I had been robbed at gunpoint.

The *after* vexations began when Diego came to my shop.

During the interlude, I paid my mortgage and whittled $3,000 off the bill from Consuela Sanchez's kidney doctor. That left me with a good chunk of the $10,000 from the "fire sale," but I was holding on to it in case I needed to stretch it out.

I spent the days reading and minding the shop. I spent three nights at Sharice's condo. She reciprocated by gamely spending one night at my place even though my only bed is a single. It turned out not to be a problem because she is so delightfully wispy.

And it was nice being so close. Life was perfect during my interlude.

Then Diego showed up.

His hair is oiled and combed straight back, no part. His skin is medium brown and flawless. His fingernails are manicured. As far as I have been able to observe, all his suits are dark blue, all his shirts white with French cuffs and all his ties of yellow silk.

Or maybe he owns only one outfit.

His manners and diction are as perfect as his grooming.

"Good afternoon, Mr. Schuze. Ms. Po requests the pleasure of your company if you are free this afternoon."

"At what time?"

"At the time of your choosing."

"Let me get a coat and tie."

Faye Po's two-story home on Silver Avenue is an architectural Oreo—traditional dark adobe on the outside, stark white on the inside. The old wood floors were scraped and bleached. The walls and ceilings are solid white. Even the hand-carved and hand-painted vigas were coated in white. A shame when you think about the craftsmen who originally painted them, but it does create a striking effect.

Across from the double pocket doors that lead into the parlor is an ornate mantelpiece carved from a single piece of jade. Above the mantel is a niche of the sort that is common in old adobe buildings. I glanced briefly at the Tompiro pot I'd sold her last year.

On the walls to the left and right are family portraits, old women seated in stiff chairs, bound feet flat on the floor, hands inside their garments. Men in flowing robes and strange hats, each hair of their sparse goatees drawn with precision.

The chairs of heavy brocade in dark hues of green and blue seem to anchor the otherwise gossamer room, preventing it from floating away. A red candle flickered on the table next to her chair.

It reminded me of a poem from a book Ms. Po gave me and that I recently thumbed through again before giving it to Sharice, who likes Zen poetry.

My visits to Faye Po are like adventures in a stream-of-consciousness novel. She nodded to me as I entered. "Good afternoon, Mr. Schuze. Thank you for coming to visit an old woman."

I walked to her chair and accepted the proffered hand.

"Vermilion candles shining on white hair."

"A line from Li Po," she noted. "Most appropriate. Will you have tea?"

I nodded and Diego poured. In addition to the tea, there were small cakes, filled with smashed fruit I did not recognize, tasting faintly of a cross between date and green pea.

At my request, she told me a story of her girlhood on the banks of the Pearl River in Guangdong. Her stories always sound apocryphal and have Aesop-esque lessons.

"A very old man—a stranger—came to my village hoping to find the graves of his ancestors. He came to my house because my father was the mayor. My father explained that we do not put names on the graves because everyone knows where their ancestors are buried. But the stranger's family had moved many years ago and no one in the village remembered his family or where they were buried. As the stranger gazed sadly out the window, he saw pieces of colored paper floating in the breeze. My father explained that it was a local custom for communicating with departed spirits. Then he put some of these papers in the stranger's hand and directed him to throw them out the window. They all floated to an old overgrown part of the cemetery, and my father officially declared that these were the stranger's ancestors."

I thanked her for the story and the tea. Diego poured me a

second cup. She asked if I might do her a favor. She had a new Indian pot she wanted me to examine. A note of concern in her voice told me this was more than a request to identify the pueblo or the likely date.

"I would be honored to see your new piece of pottery."

"You have already seen it. I saw you glance at it as you entered. But now you must look more closely. It is there above the fireplace."

I looked up. I heard something hit the floor and shatter. A teacup.

Mine, I realized after a moment of confusion.

I saw Diego bending down with a towel. I looked back up in disbelief at the niche.

I tried to gather my wits. "I am so sorry." I started to bend down to remove some pieces of the cup.

"Diego will see to it. Do not worry. It was not a treasured piece like those you have brought me over the years. Would you like another cup?"

"Thank you, no. I must leave. I will withhold my opinion on the pot until I have done research." I managed a smile. "And that gives me an excuse to visit you again."

"I hope you will forgive me for not walking you to the door. It is old age, not bad manners, that prevents it."

I declined Diego's offer to drive me home, in part because it's only five blocks. But mainly because I needed the solitude of a walk to digest what I'd just seen.

The Tompiro in the niche was not the one I sold to her last year.

It was my fake.

41

Sharice and Glad were becoming regulars. Tristan and Martin were there as well. Angie needed two trips to bring one round.

After the two margaritas, two Tecates, one Gruet and one pink gin were on the table, I made my startling announcement.

"It must be the original you sold her. She wouldn't get rid of that. Maybe it just looked different sitting up there in a niche," Tristan said.

I shook my head.

"He could be right," said Susannah. "Remember how I marveled that your copy looked exactly like the real one?"

"It looked like the real one from the missile range, not the real one I dug up on your ranch. And besides, she described it as her *new* pot and wanted me to examine it."

"Oh. So you did see it up close."

"No. I told her I needed to do some research before commenting on the pot."

"Why?" asked Martin.

"Because I had to think before I said anything. I didn't want to just come right out and say she bought a fake. She might feel terrible if she knew that."

"And even worse if she finds out that you, her trusted friend and pot dealer, made the thing," said Susannah.

"What worries me the most is her dealing with Jack Haggard. The guy is a gun-toting criminal."

"Just because he stole it from you, it doesn't mean he sold it to her," said Martin. "There could be a middleman."

"Maybe. But what happened to the original? Did Haggard or some middleman somehow convince her to trade the original for the fake?"

"Maybe she still has the original but in another room," Tristan suggested.

Susannah said, "Maybe she sold the original because she needed money and bought the fake because it was cheaper. Like those rich women in financial need who sell their diamonds and replace them with cubic zirconias."

"She doesn't seem to have money problems," I said. "The house is worth at least a million, and she has a gardener, a maid and Diego."

"Her Juan Hamilton?" asked Susannah.

"Maybe."

I asked for advice. They glanced at one another. Martin was the first to speak. "Tell the police she has unknowingly received stolen property. Let them handle it."

"Sounds like good advice," said Tristan.

"She'll know it was me who involved the police."

"She'll also realize you did so for her own good," he replied.

"Maybe it would be better if you tell her it's a fake and suggest that *she* call the police," said Sharice. "Calling them in without her knowledge doesn't seem fair to Ms. Po."

"Glad," I said, "you haven't said a word. What do you think?"

He scrunched his face as if it were an effort to figure out what advice to give. "It might help if I knew something about the lady in question."

"Think dowager queen. She lives in a genteel world of paintings on silk and servants pouring tea from hand-cast brass teapots."

"Who else could pour it?" said Susannah. "Ms. Po couldn't lift one of those clunkers."

"Probably true. She also has difficulty walking because her feet were bound as a child."

"So she's a recluse living happily in the past. I'd suggest, then, that the less you do the better so as not to disturb her tranquility. You have to give her a report on the pot, of course, and you don't want to lie to her. But how much of the truth does she really want? Perhaps you could tell her something true but innocuous, like the new pot and the old one were made by two different potters. If she seems satisfied with that, leave it be."

"But what about the fact that Haggard swindled her?"

"As Martin said, it could have been a middleman."

"It probably was. Haggard must have fenced the pot to someone. I can't picture him knowing about Ms. Po, much less dealing with her."

"But you can't let Haggard get away with robbing you," Susannah said.

"Whit will get him."

"Maybe not. The fake isn't worth much, and Whit follows the money."

"True. But he also likes to get felons off the street."

We kicked it around a bit longer and came to the conclusion I expected—we had no idea what the best course of action was.

We ordered a second round and changed the subject.

42

I called Whit the next morning and told him about what I saw at Faye Po's house.

"You want me to go see her?"

"What I want is for Haggard to be in prison. Have you found him yet?"

"I woulda let you know if we had."

"You tried that phone number?"

"'Course we did. It's a throwaway cell."

"Don't people have to show an ID to get a phone?"

"Yeah. And people are supposed to leave old pots in the ground. Wave some cash at the right person and you can get a prepaid phone on the spot."

"What about the handwriting?"

"We got nothing to compare it to. But we do have a fingerprint."

"How did you get his fingerprint without getting him?"

"It was on that card you gave me."

"I didn't think paper would hold a fingerprint."

"That's television crap. Anything will take a print if your hands are oily or dirty enough. But slick surfaces are better, so that shiny card had two perfect prints."

"How do you know they aren't mine?"

"'Cause they were from different hands. When we ran them, one was from Haggard. The other one was probably yours. It didn't match anything 'cause you don't have a record. Yet."

"Your department fingerprinted me when I was falsely arrested."

"And we purged those like the law requires when we let you go."

"How can I be sure of that?"

"You got a problem with it, Hubert, call the ACLU. Maybe you can keep them out of our way long enough so that we'll be able to find Haggard."

"He either sold the pot to Ms. Po or sold it to a middle-man who sold it to her. I hope you can track him down without involving her."

"Me too. She gives me the willies."

"Come on, Whit. You scared of a feeble old lady?"

"There something eerie about her, Hubert. I had to go there once when a maid had sticky fingers and again when there was a break-in. Sitting in front of her was like being at a séance. I could feel them honorable ancestors swooping around us."

So the ex-football player, ex-army MP and current APD cop was afraid of an elderly Chinese lady. I guess we all have our demons.

We agreed to leave Faye Po alone if possible, and that meant I had to take Glad's advice and tell her something innocuous about her new pot.

I didn't look forward to that. I don't think she has any spirits from the great beyond swirling around, but she does have a way of seeing through me. I wasn't sure I could pull off the say-as-little-as-possible feat if she started asking questions.

43

I walked and fed Geronimo, asked Glad to mind the shop and left in the Bronco. It was past the first of the month, so I didn't feel guilty about the request.

The Sanchezes were having a Cinco de Mayo celebration and asked me to bring my new girlfriend.

"This is exciting," Sharice said as we headed south. "The only time I get out of downtown is when I take the bus to the airport to fly to Montreal."

You already know she lives downtown. What I haven't mentioned is that Dr. Batres's office is also downtown. Which is a good thing, because Sharice doesn't own a car.

Neither do I, come to think of it. I own a 1985 Ford Bronco, a cross between a car, a truck and—for the last few years—an escapee from a junkyard, the latest dent being inflicted when Susannah's equally junky car rammed me from behind. She says it's the first time in history that the driver of the *front* vehicle was responsible for a rear-end collision.

Tristan is always after me to get a better vehicle, preferably a hybrid, whatever that is.

I don't want a new vehicle. I don't even want the one I have.

I'd like to live like Sharice, everything I need within walking distance. But it's hard to dig up old pots under the downtown pavement, so I keep the Bronco.

It was a typical New Mexico spring day, cool dry air and infinite blue sky. The roadside was speckled with Indian Blanket, Spanish Needles and Mexican Fireplant. Even the wildflowers were celebrating our heritage.

"Tell me about the Sanchezes."

"Emilio came here under the Bracero Program."

"There was something called the Embrace Program?"

"Why do you think *bracero* means embrace?"

"Because the French word is *embrasser*."

"Well, you're close. The Spanish for embrace is *abrazo*, from *brazos*, the word for *arms*. A *bracero* is someone who works with his arms, thus a laborer. Emilio came here to pick cotton."

She gave me the smile she reserves for ethnic humor. "Because the black folks refused to pick it?"

I laughed. "He went to Hatch, New Mexico. There were no black folks."

"And he eventually got a green card like me?"

"No, he became a citizen by marrying Consuela."

Then I did it again. I indirectly asked her to marry me. And just like the first time, not a single neural pathway in my brain participated in the asking.

"Would you like me to make you a citizen?"

She laughed and said, "Just like *The Proposal*, where the character played by Sandra Bullock is about to be deported back to Canada and forces her assistant to marry her so she can stay in her high-powered job in New York."

Once again, she either didn't think I was serious or was pretending not to think so.

"That story didn't work for me," I said.

"Why not?"

"Because the reason she was marrying a guy she didn't particularly like, much less love, was because she wanted to keep her high-powered job in the US."

"People in positions of power will often do anything to hang on to them."

"I know. But she wasn't a hedge-fund manager or the CEO of a software company. She was a book editor, for God's sake. Who would want to do that?"

"So Emilio married Consuela. After he stopped picking cotton, I suppose. What about her?"

"She never picked cotton."

She gave me a playful jab.

"Consuela was my nanny, although I thought of her as sort of a second mom or older sister. We left my parents' house the same year, she to get married, me to go to college."

"But you went to UNM."

"Yeah, and it's only a couple of blocks from the house I grew up in. But my parents thought living in a dorm would give me the college experience."

"In other words, they wanted you out of the house."

"Probably. It was weird. Most of the kids in my dorm were from Taos, Santa Fe, Socorro or other places within easy driving distance. They went home on weekends. It was creepy being in an empty dorm when classes weren't in session, so I also went home for the weekends. It was a five-minute walk."

She laughed. "I could walk to the University of Montreal. But most of the time I rode the subway because it was too cold to walk."

Emilio was waiting for us when we turned off US 85.

Actually, US 85 no longer exists. At least according to the federal government. They erased it from the records after Interstate 25 was completed. No, that's not exactly right either. They're still working on I-25, as everybody who has to drive on the northern stretch of it in Albuquerque knows.

US 85 was called the Pan-American Highway, running (at least in theory) from the tip of South America to the top of Canada. It entered the United States at El Paso, ran through Albuquerque and exited into Canada at Fortuna, North Dakota.

As a young kid, I thought my hometown was the center of the country because we had the intersection of the Pan-American Highway and Route 66, the two most important roads in America. Now both defunct.

Emilio stood proud and erect—despite the fact that he was next to NM 47 instead of the Pan-American Highway—and he bowed from the waist when I introduced Sharice.

"*Encantado de conocerle.* I apologize, Miss Clarke, for I do not speak English so well."

"No apology is necessary. I do not speak Spanish at all."

"Perhaps Uberto will teach you. His Spanish is perfect."

"I learned from your wife, *amigo.*"

"Yes. Please come and meet her," he said to Sharice, and offered his hand. "The path, it is not so level."

She took his hand and I followed them to the house. Consuela was waiting on the front porch. The fact that she had never before greeted me there should have tipped me off, but it didn't. I was totally surprised when, after meeting and talking briefly with Sharice, Consuela threw open the door and the sardined crowd shouted, "*¡Feliz cumpleaños!*"

It was the perfect setup. Because I was born on the fifth of May, it was easy for them to feign that Cinco de Mayo was the excuse for the party. And meeting my new girlfriend gave the surprise party additional cover.

Despite what many Americans think, Cinco de Mayo is not Mexican Independence Day. In fact, it is more widely celebrated out here in the Southwest than it is in Mexico, perhaps because many immigrants came from the state of Puebla, where a band of 4,000 Mexicans defeated the invading French Army, which had twice as many men and superior weapons.

Emilio and Consuela wanted to throw a surprise birthday party for me and a traditional celebration of the defeat of the French in 1862.

Well, perhaps not totally traditional. Yes, we had tamales and Mexican music. But after a goodly number of Mexican beers had been consumed, Emilio passed out small Mexican flags to about a third of the attendees and small French flags to the other two-thirds. Manny Chapa took off his apron and left his station at the *parilla* to serve as Gen. Ignacio Zaragoza Seguín, who led the victorious Mexicans. No one knew who led the French, so Sharice was designated as their leader on the grounds that she was the only person present who spoke French. She made me her aide-de-camp.

A line was drawn in the sand. I know that's from the Alamo, a battle the Mexican Army lost, but having a line in the sand trumped historical accuracy.

Sharice took the initiative, charging across the line and rallying her troops with shouts of *Allons-y, Attaque au Fer* and *Vive la France!*

The Mexican defenders initially fell back, but their counterattack won the day. We then gathered 'round for the surrender ceremony where Sharice solemnly handed her *tricolore* to Manny.

Her curtsy brought a roar of laughter.

44

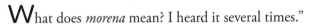

"What does *morena* mean? I heard it several times."

We were headed back on NM 47 and had just passed the intersection with NM 500, Rio Bravo Road. The Sunport was off to the right.

"It means dark."

"Is it derogatory?"

"Lupita Fuentes's mother called her daughter *mi morenita con ojos claros*—my little dark one with light eyes. Many people of Mexican descent are mestizos, so there's a lot of variation in skin tone. Describing someone often includes saying whether their skin is light or dark, but it's not derogatory. Today *morenos* sometimes means black people. Usually it's just a description. But if it's said in a certain tone, it could be racist."

"Well, I don't understand Spanish, but I can judge tone, and none of the voices sounded derogatory."

"On the contrary," I said. "I heard Manny's teenage son say to one of the Gomez twins, '*Mira a esa morena linda.*'"

"Which means?"

"Look at that beautiful black girl."

"So was Lupita one of your girlfriends?" she asked teasingly.

"Yes. She had beautiful dark skin and green eyes." I looked over at her. "I guess I went for that type even then."

"I don't remember you mentioning her when we told each other about our sexual histories."

"I was eleven."

After I left Sharice at her condo, I went to the shop to relieve Glad of his duties. I settled behind the counter with *How Georgia Became O'Keeffe* by Karen Karbo, who was listed on the cover as the author of another book called *The Gospel According to Coco Chanel*. I decided to buy a copy for Sharice.

I considered the contrast between O'Keeffe and Sharice. O'Keeffe wore no makeup and went about in flat shoes and plain shifts she sewed herself. Sharice uses lipstick and eye shadow and wears high heels and designer dresses. But those are externalities. They both have an inner strength and drive. Sharice is as dedicated to her patients as O'Keeffe was to her art.

Stieglitz's philandering sent O'Keeffe into a severe depression in 1933, but she soldiered on. Sharice's depression was caused by cancer, but she also forged ahead. In the long run, neither a bad man nor a bad disease could overcome a strong woman.

Karbo said about Stieglitz, "It's doubtful he ever had a conversation; Stieglitz was a relentless, spittle lipped monologist, commanding every room he ever entered . . . Every thought that entered his head needed to be verbalized. Here was a man who wrote at least fifty thousand letters, and *hand copied* each one before mailing it, for his records."

And I thought I was anal.

He showed O'Keeffe's early works without her permission. He took down her paintings of skyscrapers because he said men wouldn't want a woman to paint buildings. Better she stick to flowers. Oink and double oink.

I've come around to Susannah's view. Stieglitz didn't make O'Keeffe famous—he just rode her coattails.

I was so engrossed in Karbo's book and ranting about Stieglitz that I didn't look up when I first heard the bong of the door opening. When I finally did, Dotty and Donald were standing at the counter.

"Oh, Mr. Cloose, I could just hug you." She squealed and turned to her husband, "Couldn't I, Donald?"

"You could, dear."

"We just knew after our little tête-à-tête with you that everything would work out despite the tragic death of our mutual good friend Carl."

"It's good to see you again," I said, because it was my turn to say something and I had no clue what they were talking about.

"We didn't know it would happen so quickly. But we should have known, shouldn't we have, Donald?"

"Indeed we should have, dear."

"You did say 'when the time and circumstances were appropriate,' and sooner is always appropriate, isn't it?"

The question seemed directed at me, so I said, "Sooner is good."

"It is. And I can't begin to describe how happy we are with the pot. It gives our entire collection a sense of completeness."

What pot? I wondered. "I'd like to see how it fits in," I ventured.

She clasped her hands together. "We would love that, wouldn't we, Donald?"

He nodded.

"Could you come for a cocktail at five?" he said. "We can show you everything then."

"I'm already feeling thirsty. How about we make it at four?"

I was anxious to find out what pot they were referring to and why they thought it was connected with me. But not so anxious that I wanted to cancel margaritas with Susannah.

45

~

I never use the F word. And I don't like popular jargon and the abbreviations texting has introduced into the language.

But I admit my first response on seeing the pot at Dotty and Donald's sprawling home in Rio Rancho was *WTF?!*

I didn't say the words, just the letters. And I didn't say them out loud. But I would have forgiven myself had I done so, because the pot they had nattered on about in my shop that afternoon turned out to be my fake Tompiro, which had somehow migrated from the Faye Po residence in Albuquerque to the Edwards residence in Rio Rancho.

I spilled most of my Pimm's cup. I seemed to have developed a tendency in that direction. As Dotty was wiping the Saltillo tile floor with a kitchen towel and telling me not to worry about the spill, thoughts were swirling through my mind like tumbleweeds in a tornado.

Had Faye Po—with her ability to see through me—decided that dropping my teacup and beating a hasty retreat after she asked me to examine the pot were sure signs that the pot was a fake? Had she deacquisitioned it, as the museum crowd calls it? Sold it to the Edwardses?

But the Edwardses thought I had something to do with their getting it. Maybe Ms. Po mentioned me and they mistakenly thought I had urged her to sell it to them.

I declined a refill, concocted some lame story about an appointment I just remembered and headed to the Bronco. They followed me outside, thanking me profusely and asking me to return when I had time enough to see the entire collection.

When I arrived at Dos Hermanas, Susannah said, "You're right on time. I thought cocktails with the Edwardses might make you late."

"I didn't stay long." I took a deep breath. "The Edwardses have my fake Tompiro in their collection."

"I *knew* it," said Susannah. "Ms. Po's pot is the one you sold her. You just didn't see it clearly. I told you that."

"No. The pot at Ms. Po's house was the fake. I'm sure of that."

"Hmm. Okay, this must be what happened. She wanted you to tell her what it's worth because she was thinking of selling it. Since you didn't give her an evaluation, she just went ahead and sold it to the Edwardses."

"Then why did the Edwardses thank me as if I had arranged to have them get it?"

"Maybe she mentioned that she bought one from you, and they figured you had convinced her to sell it to them."

I couldn't argue with that because I'd had the same idea.

Angie arrived unbidden with our drinks, chips and salsa. I took a salty sip. Susannah just sat there thinking.

Glad showed up and said, "I closed up a bit late because another of those bargain hunters came in just before five. He didn't buy, but I think he might."

"I've got it," Susannah announced. "It's like Rudyard Whelkin, who had multiple copies of *The Deliverance of Fort Bucklow* and was trying to sell each one of them as a one-of-a-kind."

Glad asked if she meant Rudyard Kipling.

"No. Rudyard Whelkin. He told Bernie he was named after Lake Rudyard."

"Bernie?"

"Bernie Rhodenbarr, the burglar."

"He's fictional," I added.

"I seem to have come in at the middle of this conversation."

"If you'd stayed in the shop just a bit longer, you'd have been spared all of it."

The pink gin Angie brought for Glad reminded me of my drink at the Edwardses. "Have you ever heard of a Pimm's cup?"

"Of course. It's a tradition at Wimbledon. Over forty thousand are sold during the annual championship matches. They're usually served with cucumber slices."

"What is it with British drinks and cucumbers?" asked Susannah.

"Lends a healthy touch," Glad replied, "though I don't much care for them in any form."

46

I'll drive," said Thelma.

She was outside my door again, unbidden and again denied entrance because of the lit cigarette. She wanted to take me to meet Regina.

"I don't want you going back there alone after the three of us talk," she said, "so you'll need to be blindfolded."

"No way. I did that once and it turned out to be a disaster."

"Yeah. When you did that appraisal for Segundo Cantú."

"You know about that?"

"Sure. Carl was the one set it up for you. He told me all about it."

"Did he also tell you I was charged with two murders as a result? And that I could have cleared the whole thing up except I didn't know where I had been or who I'd talked to?"

"I don't think he mentioned that."

"Probably not. So I'll drive and you give me directions. Otherwise, forget it."

Not only did I not want to be blindfolded again, I didn't want to be in a car that smelled like an ashtray.

She squinted at me through the smoke. "You promise you won't go back and try to make a deal with her to cut me out?"

"I promise."

"I guess I'll just have to trust you."

"Learning to trust is important. This will be good for you."

"Hmff."

"One more thing. You can't smoke in my vehicle."

"I got a better idea. Let's walk. That way I can smoke. It's not very far."

"Then why did you want to drive?"

"I planned to go around in a few circles so you wouldn't know where we were."

"Oh, good grief. Lead the way."

We cut over to Rio Grande and walked south across Central. When we turned onto Chacoma and walked along the edge of the country club, a thought popped into my head. We were in the vicinity of the residences of both Faye Po and the Kents—Layton and Mariella.

Faye Po is a collector. Mariella Kent is a collector.

Was one of them Regina?

Thelma said she saw a Tompiro at the collector's house. I'm Mariella Kent's pot dealer. Uh, make that *pottery* dealer. I know her collection as well as she does. She doesn't have a Tompiro. So Mariella was not Regina.

And Thelma had said the collector was not named Faye Po.

Thelma must have lied. How many female collectors of ancient Native American pottery can live in one neighborhood? It had to be one of those two.

And it was. But not the one I'd reasoned it out to be.

We approached a sprawling home originally designed by El Paso architect Henry Trost, a student of Frank Lloyd Wright who did major works in New Mexico, including the Sunshine Theater, Albuquerque's first film house.

"Mariella Kent?" I said.

"You dog. I'm about to be kicked to the curb. You got to her and cut a deal."

"Remember what I told you about trust? I've known Mariella Kent for twenty years. Most of the pots in her collection came from me. But I didn't know she was the collector you mentioned until we rounded that corner. And she doesn't have a Tompiro, so you couldn't have seen one here."

"We'll see about that," she said as she hit the buzzer.

As I listened to footsteps approaching the door, another possibility came to mind. Mariella has an old pot from Acoma with black hatching on a white background. Maybe Thelma mistook it for a Tompiro.

Mariella de Baca Enríquez Kent is said to be descended from Don Francisco Fernández de la Cueva Enríquez, Duque de Alburquerque. My hometown is 91.66 percent named after him. We didn't get the first *r*.

In fact, El Duque never set foot outside of Spain. Perhaps one of his descendants did so and Mariella is a tenth-generation granddaughter.

Even if she is not descended from Spanish royalty, she has a regal bearing and more class than the average European royal. Of course, in light of the events of recent years, that is faint praise.

Mariella led us into the room where she displays her pottery. The old Acoma pot was where it's always been. The Tompiro was about eight feet to the left and on a higher shelf. So Thelma did know a Tompiro when she saw one. Well, I thought, she was married for some years to a pot hunter.

"I told you she had Carl's Tompiro," Thelma said, rather loudly. She was certain Mariella and I were in cahoots.

Mariella said, "Let me again express my condolences for your loss. As I mentioned the first time you came here, I did not enlist your husband to procure a Tompiro pot for me. I did meet him the one time I mentioned to you. He came to ask if I would sell him my Tompiro. I told him it was not for sale."

"If you didn't get it from Carl, where did you get it?"

Mariella looked at me. "I know this must be a bit of a shock for you, Hubie."

"Yes. I told Thelma you didn't have a Tompiro, but now you do. And of course I recognize it. I dug that pot up twenty years ago not far from Willard. It sat in my shop until last year when I finally sold it. How did it end up here?"

"The person you sold it to sold it to me."

"That's a drummed-up story if I ever heard one. Carl didn't come here to buy a pot, he came here to sell one."

"Why would we drum up a story?" I asked. "If Mariella bought it from Carl, she has nothing to gain by denying it."

"Sure she does. You two figured out where the fifty thousand went . . . wait, now I get it." She stared at Mariella. "You never paid him. That's why I can't find any trace of the money. He delivered the pot and you told him you'd pay him later. Then when you found out he was dead, you figured you just saved yourself fifty thousand dollars. So you two cooked up a cover story about Hubie digging up the pot and selling it to someone who sold it to you."

"I have a copy of the sales contract in my shop," I said.

"Which you probably drew up after I came to see you."

"Get a grip, Thelma. Remember that trust thing? The contract was signed and dated by both me and the buyer, and it was drawn up by my lawyer."

"Sure it was. Does this lawyer have a name?"

He did, of course. The same one as Mariella. Rather than make the situation worse by telling Thelma the lawyer was married to the woman she had just accused of swindling her, I said nothing.

My silence just increased her distrust and frustration.

"There's another possibility." She looked at Mariella again. "Maybe you killed Carl to get out of paying him."

47

When Sharice told me she was preparing moules à l'Indienne, I flashed back to the gastric episode I'd experienced at Chuy's Mexican Mariscos.

I learned the few French words I know from working in a restaurant and reading cookbooks, so "moules" struck fear in my innards.

The scent of fresh-baked bread filled the condo. I watched Sharice line up ten small ceramic bowls containing mussels, minced shallots, crushed garlic, sliced ginger, chopped cilantro, salt, pepper, ground coriander, champagne and something that looked like the runt of a carrot crop. The table held the crusty bread and the bottle of Gruet from which the champagne in the bowl had come.

"I like the way you have all the ingredients ready to go."

"Mise-en-place," she said.

I also knew what that meant from my restaurant days, but did I want my French limited to culinary terms?

"Should I learn French?"

She took her hands off the counter and clasped them behind my head. She brought her lips close to mine. "You planning on continuing to have your wicked way with me?"

I nodded.

"Then learning a bit of French would be good." She pulled me to her and kissed me.

"*C'est bon,*" I said when she finally let me come up for air.

I suggested delaying dinner and putting Benz on the balcony, but she didn't want to leave the mussels out too long. I couldn't argue with that.

"Why did you throw that one out? It looked fine."

"It was open."

I told my stomach to relax. The cook had everything under control.

She sautéed the shallots and ginger in a deep pan. Then she grated the carrot runt into the pan and added the garlic. Just as the garlic began to scent the room, she poured in the champagne and turned the heat to high. She added the coriander, salt and pepper. When the steam began to rise, she tossed in the mussels.

I was a bit alarmed by how soon she took them out, but they looked and smelled great. She ladled them into bowls and sprinkled them with cilantro.

We ate them with the crusty bread. Except for when I get a breakfast sandwich at the Grove, tortillas are my bread. Of course, I never eat mussels, and I didn't know there was a fish called arctic char. My food horizon was expanding.

"What was that orange thing you grated into the pan?"

"Turmeric."

"Isn't that a poem by Edgar Allan Poe?"

"No, that's 'Tamerlane.' He wrote it when he was a teenager."

"That probably explains why the meter was so bad. I remember reading it. So where have I heard the word *turmeric*?"

"At an Indian restaurant?"

"There are no Indian restaurants. There's a place called Pueblo Harvest Café inside the Indian Pueblo Cultural Center on Twelfth, but it isn't really Native American food. It's what they call Native-fusion. It's good, though."

"I meant Indian as in India. They use a lot of turmeric."

After dinner we did what I had wanted to do before dinner. All thoughts of pots vanished.

Then we played Scrabble while nibbling on Cocopotamus New Mexican Green Chile Caramel Truffles and drinking Gruet, both made right here in Albuquerque. Take that, France and India.

Benz was distracted by the empty mussel shells he was batting around. Although Sharice had cleaned them, I suspect the scent was still enticing.

She racked up eighteen points with *klaxon*.

I put *ind* to the right of her *k* and scored nine.

"A four-letter word? That's the best you can do?"

"Nine points isn't bad for only four letters."

"Five of those were from my *k*."

"I could have done a longer word, but this one reminded me of you."

She giggled. "You hoping for a second romp?"

"Of course. But you *are* a kind person. And courageous as well."

She cocked her head to the right and asked me why I said that.

"It took a lot of courage to show me your scar and to tell me about your past."

"Or lack thereof," she said, and we laughed.

"And you're kind because you did both of those things for the same reason—you wanted to spare me the shock of discovering them while we were in flagrante delicto."

"You're sexy when you speak Latin."

"You wouldn't think so if you heard Father Groas and me talking in it."

"Anyway, you're right. I didn't want you to have a heart attack the first time we had sex."

"I was willing to risk it."

"So why are you saying all these nice things to me? Are you going to propose to me again?"

"So you *did* notice?"

"It's not something a girl would miss."

"And what did you think?"

"The first time didn't count. You were much too excited to be rational."

"You're the one who met me at the door naked and dragged me into the bedroom."

"And the second time, you couched it as a joke—offering to make me a citizen."

"You didn't answer either time."

"This is my first ever courtship, Hubie. I'd like to prolong it."

48

⌒

She left early the next morning for work. I slid over to her side of the bed and drifted back to sleep in the cocoon of her warmth and fragrance.

When I awoke an hour later, I went to her kitchen. A brief study of the coffee roaster, grinder and brewer confirmed it was beyond my skill level.

I bought a coffee at the Flying Star on Silver and drank it while I walked home.

Diego showed up around eleven carrying a box, which he placed on my counter. "This is a present for you from Ms. Po. She would like to speak with you."

"I'll get a coat and tie."

"That won't be necessary, Mr. Schuze. She awaits you in the car."

I followed Diego into the street. He held the rear door of the car open for me. When I was seated, he closed the door and walked over to the gazebo.

The "car" turned out to be a Lincoln MKZ, trimmed with polished wood and smelling of leather. Its backseat was higher than a normal car's, making it comfortable for Ms. Po, who sat across from me on the spacious rear bench. She looked very much as she does in that throne of a chair in her house.

There was a box on her lap.

"My father had a Lincoln when I was a small girl. It was the only car in our village. It was called a Zephyr."

I made a mental note in case I ever got those letters in Scrabble. Twenty-three points would impress Sharice.

"I have not heard the word *zephyr* for many years. It is a wind, is it not?" she asked.

"It is."

"Confucius says, 'When the wind blows, the grass bends.'" She folded her hands on her lap and looked down. "I too bent, Mr. Schuze. Mrs. Kent admired the pot you sold to me. So I offered to sell it to her. I hope you are not displeased."

So maybe she was going to clear up the mystery of the pots.

"I am not displeased. I was happy you had the pot. You understood its hidden beauty. Mrs. Kent is like you, a person who will treasure the pot. So I am now happy that she has it." I decided to get the unpleasant part out. "Regarding the new pot you asked me about—"

She lifted one hand slightly. "It did not seem to me like the first one."

I nodded.

"Diego procured it at my request. I wanted to spare him from my concern. When I asked you about it, it was clear you saw it as did I."

She looked back up and smiled at me. "I hope you will approve of my new one."

She lifted a pot from the box. I felt lightheaded. Although

the humidity was 7 percent and the Lincoln's air conditioner was running, I started sweating.

"It's marvelous," I heard my voice say.

She smiled. She motioned to Diego. He walked to my side of the car and opened the door. I swung my feet out and hesitated, wondering if I could stand.

The pot in the box on Faye Po's lap was the one I'd dug up in the cliff dwelling and then reburied in a dune on the day the Trinity Site was opened for visitors.

Opening the box on my counter was anticlimactic. It was my fake.

49

~

I turned the sign to CLOSED and retreated to my kitchen table. Figuring out the movements of the pots was more important than selling pots.

I made a crude map with dots for the White Sands Missile Range, the Inchaustigui Ranch, Spirits in Clay, the Kent residence, the Po residence and the Edwards residence. Then, as the saying goes, I connected the dots. Red lines for the pot from the ranch, blue lines for the pot from the missile range and green lines for the fake. But first, because my brain just works that way, I calculated how many different combinations and permutations there could be.

Two hundred and sixteen if you assumed that one of the pots always had to be at one of the locations. But that assumption is flawed—they might have all been at the Edwardses' at one point for all I knew. So that raised the possibilities to 648.

I think. To tell you the truth, I was losing interest in the project, so I didn't think it through. It wasn't going to work. No amount of diagramming would solve this puzzle.

Susannah had left the brochure from the missile range. It was next to the stack of unpaid bills. I read the message about the

Memorial March being moved north for this year. It was funny in an officious way. One passage said, "Because of the move north, travel from the south gate to the starting point will take longer than normal. Plan on arriving at White Sands Missile Range by 4:00 a.m. It will be dark when you arrive."

So it's dark at four in the morning. Who knew?

I looked at the map and could sort of estimate where I had left the trail and gone out on my own to find the spot where I had buried the pot.

The back page had pictures from the range. The strange little obelisk marking the Trinity Site. A herd of oryx. The McDonald Ranch House, where the world's first atomic bomb had been assembled.

I remembered grousing to Susannah that the federal government had made a hole in my state by confiscating over three thousand square miles of land. Of course, the landowners were the real losers. All I lost was a chance to prospect for pots in the Oscura Mountains. They lost their livelihood.

In 1982, rancher Dave McDonald loaded his pickup with his niece Mary, his Samsonite suitcase, a thirty-day supply of groceries and two .30-30 rifles. They drove into the missile range, reoccupied their family's former homestead and posted signs telling the US Army to keep out. The army wisely declined to confront McDonald and his niece. The standoff ended when two members of New Mexico's congressional delegation—Sen. Harrison Schmidt and Rep. Joe Skeen—met with the McDonalds and agreed to hold hearings on their complaint that the government had shortchanged them when they paid compensation for taking their ranch.

The McDonalds had received $60,000. The property was later evaluated at over a million and a half.

I looked again at the McDonald Ranch House. Even in its newly restored condition, it hardly looked like the headquarters of a $1.5 million ranch. Although it did have a swimming pool.

Sort of. Actually, it was just a concrete cistern.

I remembered pictures of the scientists who were working on the bomb in 1945 taking a break from the desert heat to swim in that cistern.

Of course! That's where I had seen it. I opened one of the books I'd read about O'Keeffe and found the letter her friend Rebecca Strand had written to her husband—the photographer Paul Strand—while the two women were living in one of Mabel Dodge's guesthouses in Taos. The letter was dated June 1929:

> This afternoon, G. and I put on our bathing suits, connected the hose, and washed the Ford. Much shrieking with laughter and it came out shining like a new button.

The Ford was a Model A purchased by O'Keeffe. She named it *Hello*. I suspect the car washing was the day before they left on a tour to see more of New Mexico. O'Keeffe had written about the places they visited.

I couldn't solve the mystery of the pots, but I could solve the mystery of Susannah's putative O'Keeffe painting.

I called her and told her to come by my place after her lunch shift.

And to bring the canvas.

50

~

Susannah was incredulous. "Georgia O'Keeffe drove to the missile range?"

I shook my head. "It was 1929. There was no missile range at that time. She decided she wanted to see more of New Mexico, so even though she didn't know how to drive, she bought a Model A Ford. She was in Taos, living in one of Mabel Dodge's guesthouses. By all accounts, she was the worst student driver in history. She scared cattle, endangered pedestrians, drove into ditches and hit several trees."

She furrowed her brow. "But Taos is high desert. There aren't many trees."

"There were more before she started driving. But she evidently got the hang of it and set out on a long trip, which included White Sands."

"But since it was before the missile range, they just went to the National Monument?"

"It was also before the monument, which wasn't established until 1934."

She gave me one of her mischievous smiles. "So that was the year they trucked in all the white sand?"

"Yeah. They needed something to attract tourists. Guess where she stayed?"

"Knowing her, she probably slept in the car."

"She did on some nights. But she also spent some time at the McDonald Ranch."

"Was that a dude ranch or something?"

"Hardly." I handed her a picture of it.

"So she stayed in a plain house in the middle of nowhere. What is that . . . Wait!"

She unrolled the canvas. "That cistern is the one in this painting."

"Which proves it's a genuine O'Keeffe."

"It's cool that you found the thing she put in the painting, but how does that prove it's genuine?"

"We know the painting was done in part near Ghost Ranch because it was found there, and also because the cliffs in the background of the picture are there. But the painter must have also seen the cistern at the McDonald Ranch because it's also in the painting. We know Georgia O'Keeffe was in both places. But the odds that any other painter visited both those places are a million to one."

"I'm not sure about that, Hubie. I agree about the odds, but I've never heard of a painting's *provenance* being established by the artist being in the locales pictured in the painting."

"*Provenance* is a region in the South of France, right?"

She rolled her eyes. "No, that's *Provence*. *Provenance* is the pedigree of a piece of art. And the normal way of establishing it is to trace it from its current owner all the way back to the artist and ideally to have documents like bills of sale to verify everything."

"But my argument that she's the only one who could have painted it makes sense, right?"

"It does," she said without conviction.

She stared at the canvas the way you stare at something when you aren't really looking at it. She was thinking.

When she finally looked up, she was wearing that big rancher-girl smile. "The normal way of establishing provenance may not work for this canvas, but it will work for the wild square dance of the Tompiros, including all the do-si-does and changing partners."

"Huh?"

"Here's what you're going to do, Hubie. You're going to establish the provenance of each of the Tompiros. Start with the fake."

"Okay. That one's easy. I made it. Jack Haggard took it from me at gunpoint. Diego bought it from Haggard and took it to Faye Po. She brought it back to me."

"You have any documentation?"

"I can do better than documentation. I was an eyewitness to the pot's creation, its theft by Haggard, its presence in Faye Po's niche and its being returned to me."

"What about the part where it went from Haggard to Diego?"

"Obviously I didn't see that. But Haggard took it from me, and Ms. Po said Diego procured it for her, so it must have passed from Haggard to Diego."

She shook her head. "A provenance is like a chain, only as strong as its weakest link. Maybe Haggard sold it to X and X sold it to Diego. Except he didn't, because he kept the one he got from Haggard and sold a worse one to Diego. So you can't prove the fake you got back is a genuine Schuze because you don't have a complete *provenance*."

"I don't need one. I know my own work when I see it."

"Maybe. But Sotheby's wouldn't auction it off as a genuine Schuze unless they could verify the Haggard-to-Diego link."

I liked the fantasy of Sotheby's auctioning a genuine Schuze. That would cure my money woes. Of course, even if it were a genuine Schuze, it's still a fake.

"What about your O'Keeffe canvas? It doesn't have a complete provenance either."

"So?"

"So you don't have to give it to the museum."

"Professor Casgrail said I'd have to give it to them only if they said it was genuine."

"Which they can't say because there is no paperwork for it."

"But the people at the museum are experts. They know an O'Keeffe when they see one."

"And I'm an expert on my own pots. So if I need documentation, so do the museum experts. For all they know, O'Keeffe traded that painting to Baltazar's grandfather for some goat cheese. He hated modern art and threw it away. It belongs to Baltazar not only because he found it but also because he is the heir. He gave it to you, so it's yours."

"Goat cheese?"

"No? How about he gave her some of those skulls she painted? The point is, we don't know the provenance of that canvas. So instead of giving it away, you should sell it."

"The museum is not going to buy something they think they already have a claim to."

"I'm not talking about the museum. So far as we know, they have no knowledge the thing exists. You should sell it to me."

"You want to buy . . . Oh, of course. She said if she couldn't buy a pot, she would buy an O'Keeffe. You want to give it to Sharice."

"I do. But first I need enough money to buy it and also pay my bills. So I need to figure out if I can salvage any profit from this bizarre Tompiro caper."

"I told you it was a caper. But let's get back to your task. Give me the provenance of the pot from our ranch."

"I dug it up. It sat in my shop for twenty years. I sold it to Faye Po. I have a bill of sale. She sold it to Mariella. Given that her husband is a lawyer, she no doubt also has a bill of sale."

"Now, that's a solid provenance. Let's go to the second one, the one from the missile range."

"I know the two ends of the chain. I dug it up and reburied it in the sand dune. Ms. Po now has it. What happened in between is known only to God, whom I picture having a bit of a laugh and wondering if this sleight-of-hand trick is enough to make me a law-abiding citizen."

"Okay, do the second fake."

"There's only one fake."

"But you saw one at Po's place and one at the Edwardses'."

"I saw the one at Po's place on Tuesday. Remember we talked about how it got there and what to do about it that night with Sharice, Tristan and Martin?"

"And Glad."

"He came later. I think he got in at the end of the discussion. The next day, I took Sharice to the Cinco de Mayo party. Then later that day, the Edwardses arrived to thank me, and I went to their house and saw the fake. So it must have moved from Faye Po to the Edwardses that morning. They came to thank me right after they got it. Then that night I had dinner with Sharice, and the next day, Faye Po got the fake back from the Edwardses and delivered it to me."

Susannah is the only person I know who continues to look intelligent with her jaw hanging open. "You have got to be kidding me. What possible explanation could there be for the fake going back and forth like that in a three-day span?"

"It's not any crazier than a pot I buried in a sand dune at the missile range showing up in a box in the backseat of Faye Po's Lincoln Zephyr!"

"The Zephyr is the old one."

Susannah is an expert on old cars.

"Look," I said. "There are only two possibilities. Either the fake went back and forth like I said or Carl Haggard made a copy of my fake. Or maybe had someone else do it."

"That's three possibilities. You have the Edwardses' number?"

I took Donald's card out of my wallet, and she took her cell phone out of her purse.

"Is this Dotty Edwards?" Brief pause. "My name is Stella Ramsey from Channel 17. Yes, that Stella Ramsey. Oh, thank you. I'm doing a feature on rare Native American pots, and I understand you have a Tompiro in your collection." Another pause. "Excellent. If you're willing, I'd like to call you again after I talk to my producer about scheduling an interview and photo session with you. Great. You'll be hearing from me again soon."

"You sounded just like her."

"She's on TV every day, Hubie. Everyone knows what she sounds like. As you could tell from my conversation with Dotty, they still have their fake."

51

It finally came to me.

You probably figured it out much sooner than I did, but then you weren't having to deal with all the other pots.

"I'm such an idiot," I said to Susannah.

"Thinking the fake could move around like that isn't the brightest idea you ever had, but I don't think it rises to the level of idiocy."

"How about this—I made both fakes."

"And didn't remember it? That's not idiocy. That's early Alzheimer's."

"I didn't forget. I just didn't think about it because I threw the first one away."

"Why?"

"I took some shortcuts making it. Then I decided that even though I was going to leave it in the sand dune when I made the switch, I shouldn't compromise my workmanship. So I tossed it in the trash can and made a better one."

"It didn't break?"

"I didn't look to see. But if I'm right, it must not have. I'd thrown some bubble wrap in there, and that must have padded its landing."

"And someone looking for aluminum cans scavenged the first fake from your trash?"

"I don't think so." I didn't like what I was thinking. "A street person going through trash cans wouldn't know that a misshaped clay pot with crude hatch marks would be valuable, much less be able to locate the Edwardses and sell it to them."

I sat there thinking it through, trying to see if what I was thinking made sense.

"Well?" she prompted.

"I think Glad took it. He emptied the trash that day. And he's in the perfect position to sell it."

"So he sold it to the Edwardses?"

"I'm afraid so."

"But he seems so nice. And why wouldn't they have mentioned him to you?"

"Maybe he asked them not to. Or maybe they saw no reason to. After all, the normal thing for them to assume is that my shop minder tells me about all the sales he makes."

She assumed her detective-girl frown. The Nancy Drew face finally morphed into a smile. "We're going to solve this mystery."

"The mystery of how all the pots moved around?"

"That too. But we're also going to figure out who killed Carl Wilkes."

That sounded overly ambitious.

"Glad is César," she proclaimed triumphantly.

The smile slid off her face when I didn't react.

"Who is César?"

"The murderer in *The Flanders Panel*."

"The book with the chess stuff in it?"

"Right. Remember I told you it had a surprise ending because the murderer was someone who was always around when Julia and the chess expert were discussing the notes and trying to make sense of them?"

"I still think my vampire twist would've been a better surprise."

"I know you like to make fun of murder mysteries, but try to be serious just this once. I think we can work this out."

Her expression brooked no dissent.

"You said Glad was in the best position to retrieve your first fake from the trash and sell it. He was also in the best position to receive the real Tompiro from the missile range. Let's assume that whoever dug it up brought it to the shop when Glad was behind the counter. Would he have known to buy it?"

"Yeah. I told him all about it the morning after we got back from the range. He later reached the same conclusion you did, that Wilkes followed us and dug it up."

"See, just like César. Glad was getting inside information. So someone shows up with the pot. Did he know Wilkes had offered thirty thousand for it?"

I shook my head, not as a negative answer but as a sign of disgust. "Yes, I told him that too."

"So Wilkes gives Glad the thirty thousand. Wilkes sells it to Diego for fifty, cutting you out of the deal."

I thought about her scenario for a few seconds.

"Wilkes was like Thelma—not very trusting. I can't see him handing over thirty thousand in cash to a guy who just happens to be minding my shop. He would have waited to deal with me directly."

"Okay. Maybe it wasn't Wilkes. It must have been the MP."

"We already dismissed that possibility, remember? Unless he

figured anyone who pees on his pants is a pot thief, he'd have no reason to think I buried anything."

"Let's walk this cat forward," she said.

"What does that mean?"

"Detective talk, Hubie. You buried the pot. You splashed some water on your pants. You told the MP you couldn't hold it any longer and that's why we stopped. He asked to see your ID. You showed him your driver's license. He checked it against his list. We left the range . . . Wait—that's it! The MP dug up that pot. We were wrong to think he had no reason to go look around where you had been. He had a very good reason. You weren't on that list. He created it at the Trinity Site, remember? He added my name when I arrived. But you never went to the site. So when he compared your driver's license to the list and saw you weren't on it, he knew you'd been prowling around all day. And when he glanced at your pants, it wasn't the wet spot he was interested in. It was the canteen and the binoculars. He may not have known you were a pot thief, but he knew something was fishy."

She was right that I make fun of her attempts to apply detective fiction to real life, but in this case it worked. Not the Glad/César part—I wasn't buying that. But the walking-the-cat part. All she had to do was just list all the facts and see where it led.

"So," she continued, "he walks down the path you had come from just to look around. He spots the rebar. He digs under it out of curiosity and finds the pot."

"Okay, I can buy that. But then what?"

"It's not any trick to find you—he saw your name and address when he looked at your license. He goes to the shop hoping to sell you your own pot."

"Some might quibble about it being mine."

"Not the MP. An old pot is hardly a threat to national security. So he figures to pick up some easy money. He finds Glad instead of you. The MP has nothing to hide, so he puts the pot on the counter and asks if you're around. Glad says no but he can transact business on your behalf. So Glad buys the pot and kills Carl Wilkes."

"What? How did the *killing Carl Wilkes* part get in there?"

"I'm way ahead of you, Hubie. Carl comes in and Glad tells him he has the pot and will sell it to him for—say for the sake of argument—twenty-five thousand, thus saving Carl five thousand. But only if Carl promises to say nothing to you about it. Carl rejects the deal. He either tells Glad he's going to tell you about the offer or maybe Glad was just afraid he would, so Glad kills Carl to shut him up."

"I don't know, Suze. You're the one who said I tended to overlook Carl's dark side. Now you're saying he put principle above money. And why would Glad commit murder just to keep from being embarrassed when I found out he tried to cut me out of my own deal? It's not illegal for him to buy a pot someone brings to the store. Unethical maybe, but not illegal."

"There was a lot more at stake than embarrassment. Glad knew the pot was worth big bucks. He killed Carl for the money. Which he got when Haggard came to the shop. Jack didn't have any scruples about cutting you out of the deal. So Glad got twenty-five thousand for the pot, and Haggard made the same amount when he sold it to Diego."

"If Haggard got the pot, why did he come to my shop asking about it?"

"Maybe he didn't know Regina's name and was hoping Carl had told you."

It was all speculation, of course. But it made sense.

Then I remembered trying to show Fletcher the picture of Haggard.

"Let's look on the computer."

The way it works . . . no, I don't know how it works. I just know what happens. I lift the screen and the laptop displays a list of dates and times starting from the most recent. Double-clicking on a date/time opens the picture snapped at that moment. I have to be careful not to click anything else. Doing so causes all manner of messages to pop up on the screen, most of them announcing that updates are ready to be installed for various programs that may or may not be related to the program Tristan installed to display the photos. I hit the X's on the upper-right corners of the boxes until all of them disappear. I probably have the most out-of-date computer in New Mexico.

The first time on the list was fifteen minutes ago, Susannah caught in full stride in the doorway after I buzzed her in.

The damning photo was about three weeks earlier of a lean and hungry young man with an erect bearing and close-cropped hair.

"The MP," said Susannah.

The snapshot was dated the day after we returned from the Trinity Site open house. The guy had wasted no time cashing in on his find. I had been out running errands.

Carl Wilkes arrived later on the same day. Well, we already knew that because Glad had reported it. Carl knew I'd gone for a pot and was hoping I had returned with it.

Haggard arrived the next day. His departing photo was just his back. He appeared to be reaching for the door with both hands. Maybe he had something between his hands. Maybe not.

Typical of technology. I was now in possession of the useless knowledge that Haggard had not carried a pot *into* my store. And had no idea if he had carried one away. Maybe I could get Tristan to mount the thing in a tree across the street so we could see people as they leave.

But regardless of who carried the pot away and when, it substantiated most of Susannah's theory. I had hoped Jack Haggard was the bad guy. But now it seemed more likely that Glad was the murderer and Jack just a thief.

A deep sadness settled over me. Carl Wilkes had died protecting our friendship.

Followed by an equally deep fear. Gladwyn Farthing was dangerous.

Susannah called Whit Fletcher and explained her theory. He thought it was enough to justify questioning Glad.

When she hung up, I told her I was leaving to avoid seeing Glad.

"You should confront him, Hubert, not slink away. He killed your friend."

"That's why we have police, Suze. To confront murderers so we peaceful types don't have to. Carl was shot. For all we know, Glad carries a pistol in his pocket. Confronting him could be deadly."

"Maybe you're right. We should skip the cocktail hour tonight."

"What if he shows up there looking for us?"

"He'll be alone as he enjoys his last drink as a free man."

I thought that was a bit melodramatic but didn't say so. I went directly to Sharice's condo even though we didn't have a date. She welcomed me as enthusiastically as she does when she expects me.

She wasn't prepared to cook for us, so she suggested we give Blackbird Buvette a second try.

The green chile stew was excellent. Sharice liked her green apple and walnut salad. The Gruet was cold and crisp.

James Mintars, the menacing black guy, walked over to our table and extended his hand. I took it.

"I was out of line. I apologize."

"Accepted."

He nodded and walked away.

I rubbed the hand he had crushed.

"A man of few words," I said, and Sharice laughed.

52

⁓

I approached Spirits in Clay with trepidation the next morning. I wondered if Glad was lurking inside.

Which sort of demonstrates why I was afraid to confront him. I don't possess that kind of nerve.

I let myself in quietly and listened. Silence.

A piece of paper on the floor just inside the door read, "*Hubie—see the hoarding.*"

Was it written to me or about me? Either way, it was as cryptic as one of Faye Po's sayings.

I tiptoed to the counter. No one was crouched behind it.

I opened the door to the workshop. He wasn't waiting for me with one of my clay knives raised above his head. Nor was he in the residence in back.

I went to the shop he rented. He wasn't there either. I guessed he was in jail.

No progress had been made on the shop. There were no plimsolls. No jumpers or swimming costumes. Nor any shelves to display them on.

I felt stupid. I had missed the obvious fact that the shop was a ruse. He was not in the retail business. He was in the con-man business. And I had been his mark.

In retrospect, there had been clues. I'd met him at the Business After Hours event when he got in line directly behind me. Was it really a coincidence? He offered to rent my shop for the exact amount I was paying for it. Another coincidence? He was the one who offered to mind the shop for a reduction in the rent. Now I knew why.

I returned to my shop and took inventory, fearful that he had fled with as many pots as he could carry. Maybe that was what the word *hoarding* referred to—he was taunting me now that he was gone.

But all the pots were still there.

Also there—still taped to the counter—was the list of the thirteen people who had adopted one of my pots in hopes of eventually buying it. I called the one who had bought the Anasazi with the crooked bottom and the small crack.

When I identified myself to him, he said he was busy and abruptly hung up.

What a dunce I'd been. I'd actually felt grateful when Glad told me he'd sold that pot for ten thousand. It was marked at thirty, but I was happy to get the ten.

Until now. Obviously he got more than ten. Fifteen, maybe twenty. And pocketed the difference. The buyer gave him a check, which Glad passed on to me. And the buyer also gave Glad five or ten thousand in cash.

So he skimmed maybe ten thousand off the sale of the Anasazi. And twenty-five thousand from Haggard for the real pot if Susannah's guess was right. At least thirty for the fake if the Edwardses believed it was real. And how did he know about the

Edwardses? Because I had told him about them, of course. Just like I told him about Carl and about the Tompiro being buried because of the MP being with Susannah by the side of the road.

There's a reason why our knees don't bend back a full one hundred and eighty degrees. God knew we'd kick ourselves in the ass if they did.

The Edwardses tapped on the door. I didn't have the energy to walk over there, so I used the remote to buzz them in.

Dotty placed a box on the counter. The way things had been going, I expected her to pull out the Tompiro from Susannah's ranch. Or the Holy Grail, for that matter.

But what she lifted out of the box was a good deal less dramatic—the first fake I had made. The one Glad had sold them. Well, I thought to myself, at least this makes sense. Susannah had figured it out.

"Mr. Crozen, Donald and I are very disappointed in you, aren't we, Donald?"

"We are," he said.

I had given up correcting her various versions of my name. "I'm rather disappointed in myself too."

"Well that's refreshingly forthcoming of you. We thought you would deny it."

This was shaping up to be another typical Edwards conversation. "You thought I would deny being disappointed in myself?"

"No. We thought you would deny that this pot is a fake."

"It *is* a fake. Why would I deny that?"

Her eyes widened. "Because you sold it to us as the real thing."

"I did not sell it to you."

"Well, not directly. But you sent your employee to sell it to us."

"Did he tell you that?"

"Of course. And he also told us not to mention it to you because you were doing us an anonymous favor in Carl's memory."

That was the best line Glad could come up with? "But you did mention it to me."

"Very discreetly. We didn't say anything about the purchase. But we thought the least we could do was thank you, didn't we, Donald?"

"I believe 'the least we can do' were your very words, dear."

"But now we know why you didn't want anything mentioned. It was because you were selling us a fake."

I looked at her. "Ms. Edwards." I looked at him. "Mr. Edwards." I paused briefly. "I did *not* sell you this pot. It is a fake. I know that better than anyone because I made it. But I was not satisfied with it. I discarded it. The person who brought you the pot is not my employee." I decided not to get into details. "He is another shopkeeper who volunteered to occasionally mind my shop when I am gone. He retrieved the fake pot from my trash without my knowledge."

"But you saw it when we invited you for cocktails. Why didn't you say something then?"

I could see that not going into details might be difficult. "I saw another fake at another person's house. When I saw yours, I assumed that you had acquired it from that other person."

"Good heavens, Mr. Crozen. How many fakes did you make?"

A reasonable question.

"I intended to make only one. The first one didn't turn out as well as I hoped. So I discarded it and made a second."

Dotty's lips began to tremble. "So you have so little regard for us as collectors that you thought you could pass a fake off to us that was so bad you threw it away?"

She began to sob.

"There, there, dear," said Donald, handing her his handkerchief.

"I did *not* sell you that pot. I did not authorize anyone to sell it to you. I thought it was in the trash. I have the utmost regard for you as collectors."

Three of those sentences were actually true. I couldn't resist asking how much they paid Glad.

"We gave him a check for thirty thousand," Donald said.

My heart sank. I pictured each of those thirty thousand dollars with little wings, flying in formation behind Glad, who not only looked like Porky Pig but also was a real swine.

"Of course, I put a stop order on the check as soon as we discovered the pot was a fake."

My heart resurfaced. Then I remembered my training as an accountant. "Stop orders are sometimes missed."

"Not when the check is that large and drawn on the account of an important customer," he said with confidence.

"We still have the money," said Dotty. "Can you sell us the real one, Mr. Crozen?"

"Please," I replied, "call me Hubie."

53

Maj. Marvin Owens looked at the lean and hungry face I had cropped from a printout of the picture of the MP entering Spirits in Clay.

"Pfc. Harland Wills. What is your interest in him, Mr. Schuze?"

I had given Major Owens my actual name. It's hard enough to get on the missile range using your real name. Getting on under an alias is impossible.

"I attended this year's Trinity Site open house. When I got back home, I realized I had dropped my stepfather's railroad watch. That watch means a lot to me. My stepfather willed it to me. One of the MPs—did you say his name is Wills?—evidently found it. He brought it to my shop in Albuquerque. I wasn't there at the time, so he left it with the person who was minding the shop. I was thrilled to see that watch again. I thought it was gone forever."

"And you want to thank him?"

"I do. He must have gone through a good deal of effort to track me down, since the only identification on the watch is 'Mortimer Mosley' engraved on the back."

"Your stepfather's name?"

"Yes. I want to thank Private Wills in person. And unless there is some regulation prohibiting it, I'd also like to give him a reward."

"Although thanking him in person is a fine gesture, it may not be possible. As you probably know, we do not allow civilians to travel around the range, and I can't call him away from his duties for—"

"Oh, I didn't expect to see him *here*." I handed him a card. "I was hoping he might come to my shop when he has leave time. The name of the woman who was with me that day is written on the back of my card. The two of them chatted for a while and he might remember her."

"Is that how you came to have his picture?"

"Yes. She took his picture."

"The use of cameras is strictly prohibited at the Trinity Site."

"She didn't have a camera. She used her cell phone."

"It is the taking of pictures that's prohibited, not the devices."

"Will you give my card to Private Wills?"

He said he would. The MP who had brought me to Major Owens took me back to the gate.

It was not the Stallion Gate on the north perimeter of the range. That one is open to civilians only once a year for the Trinity Site event. I had to use the main entrance off US 70 between Las Cruces and Alamogordo. I try to avoid freeways, but Interstate 25 runs directly from Albuquerque to Las Cruces and is the fastest route, an important consideration in this case because I was making the round-trip in one day.

I broke the return leg up by stopping at Black Cat Books and Coffee in Truth or Consequences for one of each. A book and a coffee, that is. I had abandoned truth with my fictional stepfather and I didn't want to risk consequences of any type.

I asked Rhonda, the owner, if she had a copy of *The Gospel According to Coco Chanel*. She knew exactly where it was. When she handed it to me, I saw that Karen Karbo had subtitled the book *Life Lessons from the World's Most Elegant Woman*. Obviously, Karen doesn't know Sharice.

The coffee was stout enough to stand up to the freshly baked green chile scone.

The Rio Bravo art gallery is just a few feet from Black Cat, situated in front of a small triangular median created by the intersection of Broadway and Riverside. The median is like a mini park with trees, benches and three parking spaces, one of which held the Bronco.

I walked behind the gallery and watched the greenish-brown water of the Rio Grande, its current swift owing to releases from Elephant Butte Dam three or four miles to the north. Despite its name and its crucial role in a state that is mostly desert, the majestic river receives little attention and even less fanfare.

I took a look in the gallery to see if they had an O'Keeffe. They didn't. But a showing of works by an artist named Susan A. Christie caught my eye because she titled them *The Pentimento Series: Ink & Gouache on Japanese Paper*.

54

~

"You made a round-trip to the south end of the missile range and still made it back in time for margaritas?"

"A man needs priorities. Having margaritas with you trumped sleeping late. So I left at seven and got back five minutes ago."

"Ten hours behind the wheel. You must have hated it."

"Eight hours. I spent an hour at the missile range and an hour at Black Cat."

"I love that place. Did you stop by the gallery?"

I told her I did and handed her a catalog of the show by Susan A. Christie. "You know anything about her?"

"Sure. She's well known in New Mexico. There are lots of similarities between her and O'Keeffe. Both were raised in the Midwest. Both visited New Mexico, where their painting became more experimental and full of vibrant colors. And both ended up moving here. Christie is also influenced by Chinese art. She studied with Cheng-Khee Chee—"

"*Gesundheit.*"

"Ha-ha. She was also one of the first Westerners to attend the Zhejiang Academy of Art."

"What does *gouache* mean?"

"It's *gwash,* not *gwáchee.* It's like watercolor but opaque."

"You told me *pentimento* is when you can see part of an older painting under a new one. How can she accomplish that using opaque paint?"

"You can mix *gouache* in different levels of opacity. But judging from the pictures in this catalogue, I'd say she's just using *pentimento* as an inspiration. Technically, you can't paint one. But you didn't drive all the way down there to look at paintings and drink coffee. What did you do at the missile range?"

I told her what and why.

"I didn't take a photo," she protested. "They told us when we registered at the site not to take any."

"I know that. But I didn't want to say my security system had surreptitiously snapped his picture."

"You think he'll come back?"

55

He did, but his greeting didn't bode well. "I could arrest you for trespassing in a high-security zone. And looting a protected site."

"You'd have a hard time explaining why you waited so long. And regarding the looted site, you'd have an even harder time explaining why you were the one who sold the looted pot."

"You can't prove that."

I placed his snapshot on the counter.

"Where'd you get this?"

I pointed to the front of the shop. "Everyone who comes through that door is photographed."

"So I was shopping."

"Then why does the next picture show you putting the pot on this counter? My customers don't bring pots. They leave with them."

It was another lie, of course. For a good cause. But still a lie. I sounded so convincing that I feared I was getting good at it.

He was thinking now instead of talking, no doubt reassessing the blustery approach he had planned. "Why'd you want me to come back?"

"Because my counterman shorted you, and I want to make it right. In return for which I want a favor."

"You videoing this meeting?"

"No. And if I did, I'd be putting us both in jail. You want to hear the deal?"

"Sure."

"What did my counterman give you for the pot?"

"A thousand dollars."

Just the amount I had guessed. *Thousand* has a sort of gravitas that *five hundred* lacks. Or *nine hundred* for that matter. For a guy earning a private's wages, a thousand is a big score. Glad was crafty.

"The pot was worth six thousand. I'll give you the five he shorted you."

Another lie. And I went all the way up to five because I didn't want to lose him for a few measly thousand when there was ten times that much at stake.

"What's the favor?"

"Get me in the range."

"No way."

"You know all I want is another pot. I'm not a spy. I'm not interested in sensitive areas or equipment."

"Security is way too tight. I couldn't do it even if I wanted to."

So he had switched from *no way* in the sense of there is no way I *will* do it to *no way* in the sense of there is no way I *can* do it. I had him.

"Just listen to the plan. WSMR 311 meets the eastern boundary of the range less than half a mile from US 54."

"That junction is closely monitored," he noted.

"Doesn't matter. You ever work that area?"

"Sometimes."

"Call me the next time you'll be there at night. If you're alone, hike south. If you're not alone, tell the other guys you want to take a smoke, answer the call of nature or whatever. You'll see an arroyo half a mile away. It's about eight feet deep. Put a red bandana on the ground where the FP2100-X perimeter intrusion cable runs. Put a rock on the bandana so it doesn't blow away."

"If you're not involved in espionage, how do you know about the FP2100-X?"

"I read about it in the *Alamogordo Daily News*."

"Oh. Then what?"

"Make sure none of your buddies go down there for at least twenty minutes."

"That's it?"

"Yep. After twenty minutes, I'll be well away from the perimeter on my way to where I hope another pot is buried."

"When do I get the money?"

"Come to my place two days after you leave that bandana."

"How do I know you'll pay?"

"You'll have to trust me."

He thought about it for a few seconds. Then he said, "Gimme your number."

56

It was only three days until he called, but it felt longer.

Fletcher had come by to say they hadn't been able to locate Glad. So he wasn't in jail as I had speculated. He was simply on the lam.

Then Fletcher said they also hadn't found Jack Haggard.

"How about Amelia Earhart?" I asked.

He was not amused.

Thelma came by twice. She said she was working on the trust thing.

The Edwardses also came by twice. Dotty brought cookies the second time.

I called the guy who cut the deal with Glad for the Anasazi with the crooked bottom and the small crack. He tried to hang up quickly, but I cut to the chase while he was saying he couldn't talk to me at that moment.

"I know you paid cash to my counterman to get a discount. Bring me five thousand, and I won't report your scam to the police."

He made a lewd suggestion and hung up.

Shoot. I was hoping to use his five thou to pay Private Wills in case I couldn't close the deal with the Edwardses fast enough to pay him within two days of getting the new pot.

Or in case there wasn't another one where I found the first one. But since the site had never been explored save for my one brief visit, I was hopeful there would be.

Before I left, I stopped by La Placita, where Susannah was working the lunch shift.

"You here for lunch?"

"Just a La Placita Burger to go."

It has green chile.

"Where are you headed?"

"The missile range."

"So Wills called?"

"Yeah. I'll be on the east side of the range south of Carrizozo. He'll mark the spot where I'll cross the FP2100-X gizmo. I'll go to the site, hopefully find something and be out of the range before sunup."

"Happy hunting."

When you drive along US 54 south of Carrizozo, you see more antelopes than cars. And that's during the day. After dark, you could pitch a tent on it and get a full night's sleep.

I chose to drive off the road and spend the time in the cozy confines of the Bronco, using my new night-vision binoculars to watch the arroyo I had described to Wills.

He arrived shortly after eight and placed the bandana. I don't know if it was red. Everything seen through the night-vision binoculars was green.

I drove as close to the boundary as I could get.

The multipurpose folding ladder is only six feet long when folded, so it fit easily in the Bronco. The ladder's four sections can be set at a variety of angles. Line them all up and you have a twenty-four-foot straight ladder to lean against a wall. Fold it in the middle and you have a twelve-foot stepladder. The configuration I used was the two end pieces at ninety degrees and the two middle pieces level between them, forming a bridge six feet tall and twelve feet across.

I stood the bridge up on one of its legs and hooked the Bronco's winch cable to the leg sticking up in the air. I had practiced it on a deserted side road on the way down, so I was able to let it down gently.

Was I detected? Did the very slight vibration of the ladder as I stepped on it trigger something? Did they have a supersensitive seismograph in addition to the FP2100-X? Was it a trap? Were Wills and his buddies watching, ready to apprehend me?

I had no answers, so I set off at a trot and continued along the arroyo for twenty minutes. At which point I was almost two miles away from the perimeter.

I stopped to get my breath, then started walking.

The moon was in the same ecliptic longitude as the sun and therefore invisible. As an amateur astronomer, that's the way I think of it. You probably call it a new moon.

At any rate, the only light was from the stars, but I somehow found my way.

I did stop and use the night-vision binoculars from time to time just to scan the horizon for structures, none of which were anywhere near my path.

I reached the cliff dwelling around eleven. Although the hidden path to the dwelling climb was not terribly steep, it was narrow. I decided not to risk it in the dark.

I unrolled my sleeping bag under a piñon pine. The tree

seemed to be pointing me toward the cliff dwelling. I thought about another tree I had gazed into on a cold and snowy night at the D. H. Lawrence Ranch. It stood sentinel in front of Lawrence's cabin. I had walked to the cabin for the same reason I had walked to the base of this mountain. There was a pot that needed rescuing.

Or stealing, if you want to be cynical.

O'Keeffe painted the tree at the ranch and titled it *The Lawrence Tree*. Her directions for hanging the picture say to stand the tree on its head. Which is more or less what she did to the art world.

O'Keeffe wrote that she would lie under the tree and stare into the branches. The tree in her painting doesn't look much like the one I saw. For one thing, she made the trunk pink. Artistic license?

Or maybe she actually saw it that way. When she taught at West Texas State Normal College in Canyon—now known as West Texas A&M—she painted landscapes of Palo Duro Canyon. Palo Duro means "hard stick" in Spanish.

After showing one to a local resident, he said, "That doesn't look like the canyon."

"I painted it the way I felt," she replied.

"You must have had a stomachache," he said.

As Susannah frequently notes, "Everyone is a critic."

I awoke before five. There was faint light behind the mountains. My change of plan had put me in a time bind. I wouldn't be going back to the Bronco under cover of darkness. But I figured if I got there early enough, I could have the ladder folded up and be on the road while most people were showering or having breakfast. And it wasn't as if anyone would be walking around where I'd parked. It wasn't a road and it wasn't visible from the highway.

When there was just enough light to see the trail, I started up.

The place was exactly as I had left it except the remortared wall had dried and looked as though it had been there forever. I had repaired the partially hidden space immediately after digging up the pot.

What else was back there? A line from Poe's "Tamerlane" came to mind—"more than crime may dare to dream."

And that's what I found. Another intact pot, enough pieces of a second one to glue together in a way collectors like, a variety of other shards and a beautiful mole fetish. Moles were revered for their sense of direction in the dark.

As I rolled the pot and shards up in my sleeping bag to protect them, I thought about Faye Po's story of the stranger seeking the graves of his ancestors. No one ever would come here seeking their ancestors. These people are gone forever.

I felt good about coming back.

The mole fetish would be valuable in my shop. But I left it in the cave that bore its name. It had been more valuable there. Guiding my footsteps under a moonless sky.

57

~

You may recall my concern that the guys in the black helicopter might think my claim to be digging up pots was just a cover for espionage, since it was the third time I'd gained unauthorized entry.

If you've been counting, you know what happened next.

I had descended from the cliff and slipped between two large boulders. On the other side of those stones was the east slope of the Oscura Mountains, my route back to the ladder and the Bronco. All I had to do was keep walking.

Then I heard the roar and saw the rotating blades.

My rapid retreat back through the boulders was obscured by the sand kicked up by the copter's landing. I was back in the cliff dwelling when they started searching for me, protected only by the cleverly hidden path built by the Tompiro, some tall grama grass and a little carved mole.

The two soldiers in camo gear split up after they cleared the passage between the boulders. I relaxed a bit when the one who came my way sprinted past my perch. But he had returned and was scanning the terrain with his binoculars.

I turned on my fancy binoculars and aimed them at him. In

the movies, this makes people blind. Tristan had told me that can't happen. What he had not told me was why. The answer is that the damn things shut down automatically if they get too much light.

Now you understand why I don't rely on technology. From the automated camera on the shop entrance to the night-vision binoculars, they always fail you when you need them the most.

So I just stared at him with my twenty/twenties. I need glasses only for small print. Good thing the camo guy wasn't a book.

Then he did something remarkable. He put down his binoculars. He took off his helmet. He tilted his head back. He was a hundred feet below me but clearly visible.

Pfc. Harland Wills.

I scrambled down.

His pack was off when I reached him.

"You find what you were looking for?"

"Yes."

He held the pack open. "Quick, stuff it in here."

I stuffed my bedroll into his pack.

He handcuffed me.

Just to make sure all the bases had been touched, I repeated the details of the cover story I'd given Major Owens.

"Keep your mouth shut," Wills said as we passed through the boulders. "Trust me."

I had asked him to trust me. He had. So I decided I would trust him.

It helped that I had no other option.

58

~

The "Tompiro caper," as Susannah called it, had been one long string of unpredictable and inexplicable events.

It started well enough. Unearthing the pot during the Trinity Site Open House went just as we planned.

Then things began to spiral out of control. I had to bury the pot because Wills was with Susannah. It had been unearthed when I went back to get it. Carl Wilkes was murdered. My fake showed up in Faye Po's niche. Then in the Edwardses' house. Except it was the second fake. Or maybe it was the first one. If you're clear on this, I congratulate you. I can't keep it straight, and I'm the one it happened to.

Then the pot I sold to Faye Po ended up in Mariella Kent's collection. And the pot I buried at White Sands ended up with Faye Po. And my new friend Gladwyn Farthing turned out to be a thief and maybe a murderer.

So with all of that as background, I shouldn't have been surprised when they took me into an interrogation room at MP headquarters, and Glad was standing there next to Maj. Marvin Owens.

But I was surprised. Wills tightened his hand on my elbow as a reminder to stay silent. I glared at Gladwyn. He smiled at me.

"Good to see you, Hubie. You had us all worried, disappearing like that."

Wills pushed me down into a chair. The major and Gladwyn sat down opposite me. Wills remained standing behind me with his hand above my elbow, as if he would grab me if I tried to bolt. The other MP also remained standing.

I found an oddly shaped coffee stain on the table and studied it. The major explained that I was in serious trouble.

As if I didn't know that? But given the bizarre course of the Tompiro caper, I wouldn't have blamed him for thinking that even the most obvious of facts needed explaining to me.

"Mr. Farthing showed up this morning to tell us you had come down this way to hunt for artifacts. He said you told him the site was on the edge of the missile range. But when he looked at the map after you left, he realized it was *in* the range. When you didn't return last night as expected, he became alarmed that you might have wandered onto the range. He asked us to search for you."

He paused. I continued to examine the stain. With a bit of imagination you could see it as a mole. I kept trusting Wills and remained silent.

"How did you get into the range?"

Maybe not a mole. Maybe a gopher. The body was thinner.

"Well?" prompted the major.

Wills touched my arm gently with one finger. I read this as a different instruction and answered the question.

"I didn't know I had entered. I guess I just walked in."

"How did you avoid detection?"

"You're in a better position to answer that than I am. I don't know how you detect things."

He didn't follow up on that. Instead he stated that there are

ENTRY PROHIBITED signs every fifty feet around the entire peri-meter of the range—more than twenty thousand of them.

"How did you manage not to see them?"

"It was dark."

The major looked at Wills. "Do you remember him?"

"No, sir. But he must have been at the Trinity Site this year. I found a watch and finally tracked him down as the owner. I took the watch to his store and left it with a clerk. I never saw Mr. Schuze, but the clerk told me his name. So when you came to the barracks and informed us of the situation, I naturally vol-unteered to join in the search."

"And you found him. Good work, Wills."

"Thank you, sir."

"Did you search him?"

"Thoroughly, sir."

"And?"

"Nothing out of the ordinary. Binoculars, canteen, compass, wallet, car keys."

"No artifacts?"

"No, sir."

The major pointed a finger at me.

"You sure you came into the range by accident?"

I lied and said I had no idea I'd wandered onto the range.

"You show up on this base again, and I'll make sure you stay on it a lot longer than you bargained for. You clear on that, mister?"

He sounded like Jack Nicholson in *A Few Good Men.* I was surprised he didn't yell, "You can't handle the truth!"

I wasn't worried about handling it. I would have settled for just knowing it.

He kept staring at me even after I had answered. I looked down.

Gopher wasn't right either. The tail was all wrong. Then it came to me—a platypus. And I wondered what the devil a platypus was doing in New Mexico.

The major spoke to Wills. "Get him out of here."

"Yes, sir."

Wills put Gladwyn in the backseat of a jeep. He put me in the front passenger seat. We drove in silence to the main gate. My Bronco was parked just outside of it. I stared at it.

At this point, I was desensitized to surprise. If the five Avenger torpedo bombers from Flight 19, which disappeared over the Bermuda Triangle, had been parked next to the Bronco, the most I could have mustered was a yawn.

Wills opened our doors. He handed me my sleeping bag. Glad gave me my car key and took the passenger seat in the Bronco. (Compared to the enigma of Glad being on the missile range seated at the right hand of the major, the fact that there was no sign of how he got there seemed a trifling puzzle.) I walked around to the other side and got behind the wheel.

"Where to?" I asked.

"The Black Cat."

I drove from the gate to the intersection with Highway 70 and turned to the southwest toward Las Cruces.

Funny how time stretches out when you're driving along in silence with a murderous thief.

The planes from Flight 19 were not parked in front of Black Cat.

But Susannah's Crown Victoria was. Its oxidized purplish paint and rusted roof where the vinyl peeled off are hard to miss.

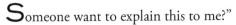

59

Someone want to explain this to me?"

We were seated on a bench in the median mini park with coffees from Black Cat. We had moved outside for privacy.

"You obviously didn't get my note," Gladwyn said.

"What note?"

"The one I slipped under your door telling you to look in the hoarding."

"That was a note? And what the devil is a hoarding?"

"The shadowbox-like thing on your shop. The place where you put the sale advert."

"Why did you put a note there?"

"The door locked behind me when I left at five. The authorities came for me shortly afterwards. I wanted you to know I wouldn't be available the next day for minding the shop."

"Why didn't you just slip the note under the door instead of slipping a note directing me to a second note using a term I never heard?"

"The note was multiple pages and had documents attached. It wouldn't fit under the door. Sorry about *hoarding*. What do you call an advert box of that sort?"

"If there's an American word for it, I don't know it. So the authorities arrested you and you left me a note before going to jail."

He shook his head.

Susannah said, "Let him tell the story."

"I was not arrested. It's a long story and, I regret to say, a painful one for me."

He sipped some coffee, then took a deep breath. "I came to this country on a tourist visa. But my real goal was to live and work here. Green cards take a long time and I possess no special work skills that would speed up the process. So I decided to aim for an E-2 Treaty Investor Visa. It's for individuals who want to start an enterprise as opposed to working for an American employer. I suppose the idea is if you start a business, you aren't taking a job from a Yank and may even end up creating some jobs. The problem is that you need to demonstrate that you are making a substantial investment in the enterprise. The Department of State recently decided that fifty thousand is enough for a small business. There are some other requirements, such as being from one of the E-2 treaty countries, showing that the investment is totally at-risk, that the investment funds did not come from criminal activity and so forth. I met all the requirements except for the fifty thousand. My plan was to start the business on the sly. I have a modest income from my superannuation scheme, enough to live on, put a bit into the business each month and eventually have enough in the bank to get the visa."

We call it a pension plan. The Brits call it a superannuation scheme, as if accumulating a lot of years is super and also a bit shady. In England, *scheme* is evidently a synonym for *plan* and lacks the negative connotation it has here.

"The day after your first visit to the missile range, Private Wills came to the shop while you were out running errands. He placed a pot on the counter and told me you had *left it* at the missile range. I realized immediately that it must be the one you had told me about, and that you hadn't merely left it, you had buried it. But I didn't say anything to Wills. Instead I offered to buy it. I knew how much you wanted that pot, so I offered him a thousand dollars for it. He took it. I used part of my savings to buy that pot. I planned to tell you about it when you returned and have you pay me back. But then Carl Wilkes came in an hour or so later. He was excited when I showed him the pot. He said he would return the next day with the cash. So I changed my mind about telling you. I wanted to wait until Carl brought the cash. It would be a great surprise for you, since you didn't even know Wills had brought your pot. I kept the pot at my place that night but brought it in the next to have it ready for Carl. It was the most unfortunate decision of my life. Carl did not return the next day. Another man did. He said he had come to pick up the pot, and Carl would be along shortly with the money. Naturally, I told him I couldn't release the pot before having the money in hand. Whereupon he pulled a gun from his jacket."

Now I realized why Glad had said "Again!" when I told him my alternative plan to his markdown sale had fallen through "at gunpoint." He wasn't referring to a gun being pulled on *me* again. He was referring to a gun being pulled first on *him*, then again on me. But he had managed to cover his slip.

Up until this point, I had assumed his narrative was just a lame story he was weaving to explain away his misdeeds. But if he had in fact been robbed by Haggard, I might have to reconsider.

"I cost you thirty thousand dollars," he said. "I should have told you about the pot the day Wills brought it."

"What difference would it have made?"

"You might have called Wilkes and sold it to him that evening. You might have hidden it. Any course of action would have been better than mine. And it gets worse. I found a pot in your dustbin. I didn't know why you tossed it away. It looked better than some of the old cracked ones you have. So I decided to see if I could sell it and recoup a bit of the money I'd lost for you. I thought the Edwardses might be interested, so I took it to them. I was gobsmacked when they offered me thirty thousand. It was so providential. I could replace the exact amount I had lost for you on the real one. But when I tried to cash the check, they had stopped payment on it. I am truly sorry, Hubie. I apologise."

You can hear the difference between the American *z* and the British *s* if you listen closely.

"Those are not the only two pots you were involved with. What about the Anasazi you sold for a third of its price?"

"I thought you were pleased about that."

"I was. Until I figured out that you actually sold it for more than that and skimmed some off the top."

His eyes widened. "I did not do that."

"I called the buyer twice and in both cases he refused to talk to me."

"It must be for some other reason. He paid me ten thousand and I gave you the check."

"No cash on the side?"

"Absolutely not."

"What about the 'authorities' you referred to who didn't arrest you?"

"They were from the US Citizenship and Immigration Services. They claimed I was running a business whilst on a tourist visa. They were right, of course, but I denied it. They did not arrest me. They asked me to go with them for questioning. So I left you a note explaining everything and even attached documents regarding the E-2 visa and information about whom to contact both at the British embassy and back home should I be ultimately detained. They questioned me vigorously even though I showed them before we departed that there is no merchandise, no sign, no cash box, nil. I told them I was living there, which is true, and they released me."

"The reason there was no merchandise, sign or cash box," I said, "was because the shop story was a ruse. You didn't rent the space to open a store. You rented it to swindle me while minding *my* store."

"No, you've got it all wrong. I haven't started the shop because the money I intended to pay Martin to fabricate display cases went to Private Wills."

I thought about it for a minute. "It appears we are stalemated. I can't prove any of what you said is false. And you can't prove any of it is true."

"Yes he can," said Susannah.

We both looked at her and said in unison, "How?"

She pulled a manila folder from her bag and five photos from the folder. They weren't technically photos because they were on copy paper from a printer. She lined them up on the sidewalk in front of the bench. I recognized all five of the men. Four of them were customers from several months ago.

She turned to Glad. "Show me which of these pulled a gun on you."

He immediately picked up one of the papers. It was not one of my four customers.

It was the snapshot of Jack Haggard entering Spirits in Clay. Not when he entered wearing the hat, obviously. It was his entrance the day he robbed Glad.

60

"Why did you send Glad to rescue me instead of coming your-self?" I asked Susannah.

"I was afraid someone might recognize my name and start asking questions. Better to send someone with no connection to anything that happened on the missile range. So I drove Glad to where you'd left the Bronco. He drove the Bronco to the range and gave them the story about being worried when you didn't come back. I drove to Black Cat to wait."

We were, of course, safe and sound back in Dos Hermanas.

Well, safe at any rate. Whether I was sound might be questioned.

I'd gone back to retrieve my ladder. It had been easy to put in place the night before. All I had to do was stand it up and winch it down. But I couldn't reverse those two steps because half of it was now inside the range. If I stood outside the perimeter and pushed it up, it would be standing entirely inside the range on the other side of the FP2100-X. And I couldn't push it from the other end without being in the range myself.

I puzzled over the geometry for a minute or two. Then I looked around. I could have been on Mars. Not a single visible human contrivance except the Bronco and the ladder.

"What the hell," I said out loud.

I attached the winch and dragged the ladder across the FP2100-X.

As I headed north on US 54, I imagined MPs in a bunker somewhere looking at a panel with strobing lights and ear-piercing beeps triggered by the FP2100-X.

Now I was sitting across from Susannah with a handful of chips and a headful of questions.

"So instead of Glad selling both the White Sands pot and the discarded pot surreptitiously, he was actually trying to do something nice by selling the first one and surprising me with the money because I thought the pot was still buried on the range. Then when he got robbed, he sold the discarded one to try to recoup the money he caused me to lose. Do any of your murder mysteries have plots like that?"

"No. They always make better sense."

"That's because truth is stranger than fiction. When we gathered at Black Cat, did you already know our theory about him was wrong?"

"He'd told me what he told you. I wasn't positive. But his agreeing to go to the range and see if he could do something made me begin to trust him."

"But you went to my computer and printed those photos just in case."

She smiled. "Trust, but verify. Now we know Glad's story is true. So why did the guy who bought the discounted pot refuse to talk to you?"

"The first time, he claimed to be busy. My guess is he felt guilty about getting the pot so cheaply after I sort of kept it in layaway for him."

"And the second time?"

"Well, I accused him of swindling me."

"That probably explains why he hung up on you."

"After making a lewd suggestion."

"Yeah, you told me. So Haggard must have killed Wilkes. Too bad Fletcher can't find him."

"Maybe he won't have to find him. Maybe Haggard will find Fletcher."

"You have a plan?"

"Remember you pretended to be Stella Ramsey when you called Dotty Edwards to see if they still had the fake?"

"I figured that name would prompt her to tell me."

"That's what gave me this idea. But instead of you pretending to be Stella Ramsey, I'm going to call the real one."

61

Charles Webbe came to Spirits in Clay the next morning just as I was picking up the phone to call Stella.

"You've been charged with murder in the past and now with trespassing at the missile range. If anyone had ever caught you digging, you'd have a long and varied rap sheet."

"The FBI keeps tabs on the goings-on in the range?"

"Since 9/11, all agencies with a role in national security are supposed to cooperate and share intelligence."

"How's that working out?"

"Working fine here in New Mexico, where we all know each other. Doesn't work at all in the District. Too much politics, too many people protecting turf." He smiled. "On the other hand, there's not much intelligence within the Beltway, so maybe it doesn't matter if they share it. Major Owens told me you didn't leave the range with anything. That true?"

I shook my head.

"I didn't think so," he said. "You've got a knack for stealing pots."

"I didn't steal anything. I just did a little prospecting. It's public land. I'm part of the public."

"What did you find?"

I retrieved the Tompiro from under the counter and set it in front of him.

"Impressive."

"I also found most of the pieces to a second pot. And a mole fetish."

"Which you left in the cave."

"How'd you know?"

He lifted his arms with his palms up to take in the shop. "Nothing but pots in here. You don't sell fetishes."

"I could have taken it anyway."

"No. Too sappy for that. How much is this pot worth?"

"Fifty thousand, but I'm selling it for thirty."

The reason, of course, is that's what Glad sold the fake to the Edwardses for. They didn't know it was a fake. So they thought they could buy a genuine one for thirty, and I didn't feel like trying to hold them up for another twenty. And thirty was all I had expected to get from Carl anyway.

"I won't ask why you marked it down. But shouldn't you keep it somewhere more secure than under your counter?"

"I have it here because the buyer is coming today. But first, there's going to be a media event."

I told him about Stella and the plan.

"Mind if I attend? You might need some muscle."

62

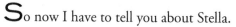

So now I have to tell you about Stella.

We met in an elevator. She said, "I'm Stella, but of course you already know that." She said the same thing when she met Susannah—and for all I know, says it to everyone she meets.

And most of them would in fact know she is Stella because they see her every day on television. She's Channel 17's Roving Reporter.

I didn't know who she was at the time, but I came to know her intimately. Literally. She seduced me. I offered only token resistance.

She may possess great reportorial skills, but we all know why she does all the "stand-ups" for Channel 17. She is gorgeous.

Our brief affair came to a sudden end when one of her stand-ups announced that a murder victim "was someone Hubert Schuze had a longstanding grudge against. Schuze was at a party in an apartment near the victim's residence. He left the party shortly before a gunshot was heard and returned covered with blood."

It was all a misunderstanding, of course—it always is—and she apologized. So we parted on good terms.

That may explain why she agreed to run the Tompiro story. Or maybe she would have run it just for the news value. It was about my "coming into possession" (a carefully chosen weasel phrase) of an intact Tompiro pot.

She stood in front of Spirits in Clay, the pot in one hand, a microphone in the other.

Charles Webbe stood behind the cameraman. Hard to attract a criminal with an FBI agent in plain sight.

After the camera was off, Stella handed the pot to Dotty Edwards. Donald handed me $30,000. I had specified cash. I handed $5,000 of that to Private Wills and $6,000 to Susannah Inchaustigui.

Charles watched. No one in the small crowd tried to make a money grab.

Susannah said, "I can't accept this, Hubie."

"Sure you can. It's your twenty percent."

"But the wager was for twenty percent of the pot you found on our first visit to the range. I had nothing to do with you finding this one."

"You had everything to do with me being able to keep it. If you hadn't concocted that story and sent Glad, I never could have gotten out of there with the pot."

"I could use the money for this fall's tuition, but it just doesn't feel right."

"Okay, how about you sell me the O'Keeffe for six thousand?"

"Deal."

The next person in my cash line was Thelma Wilkes, whom I'd called on the pretense that she might enjoy seeing Stella's stand-up.

I talked to her discreetly off to one side.

"I'm sorry, Thelma. Carl never did get that fifty thousand."

"Yeah, I know that now."

"How much do you need for your medical bills?"

"Somewhere around four thousand. You don't need a clerk, do you? I have some bad days when I wouldn't be able to come in, and I'm not sure how long I can stay in your building without smoking—"

"Thelma, I don't need a clerk."

She looked down.

"Hold out your hand."

She did so without looking up. I placed a stack of fifty hundred-dollar bills in her hand. "This is for your medical bills. Plus another thousand to enroll in a quit-smoking program or buy a lifetime supply of Nicorette."

"Thank you. I don't like taking charity, but I need the money."

"It's not charity. Think of it as money from Carl. He's the one who sent me looking for another Tompiro. Without him, I wouldn't have this to pass along to you."

The search had taken a winding path, but he was the one who prompted me to take the first step.

"I feel better now about trusting you," she said before she left.

63

Jack Haggard probably enjoyed looking at Stella Ramsey as much as do the other men in Albuquerque.

Of course, his interest in her most recent stand-up spurred something more than lust.

I'd agreed several years ago to be a decoy. Whit furnished me a Kevlar vest for the occasion, but that didn't make standing behind my counter staring down the barrel of a gun any less stressful. We had to do it that way because I needed to extract a confession before Whit stepped out from behind my workshop door to make the arrest.

This time we didn't need a confession. And not only did I not play decoy, I wasn't even in Old Town when Haggard showed up to rob Spirits in Clay for the third time.

Which turned out not to be a charm.

The first counterman he robbed was Gladwyn Farthing.

The second was Hubert Schuze.

The third was Whit Fletcher.

Who got the drop on Haggard.

Whit didn't have to reach into his jacket for his gun. It was in his hand just out of sight below the counter.

He cuffed Haggard and took him to a motel room Haggard was renting. He collected some stolen artifacts and a good deal of cash. The artifacts were confiscated as evidence. The cash was confiscated as evidence.

Some of it.

Most of it ended up in Whit's pocket. He never told me how much. He did give me a cut, even though it was not the original money we were looking for and he could have kept it all.

The other money had paid most of my bills and I still had the shards to assemble into a collector's item. So since this was money I hadn't expected, I donated it to a fund that assists the remaining survivors of the Bataan Death March.

You may remember me mentioning a bookstore here in Old Town called Treasure House Books and Gifts. The building is owned by Jim Hoffsis, a veteran. His son, John Hoffsis, runs the store. The two of them have been participating in the Annual Memorial March for years. They invite me to join them each year. I think I'll take them up on the offer next time.

I haven't yet decided if I'll stay on the trail the entire walk.

64

I didn't go back to Old Town after Haggard's arrest.

Sharice and I were in bed. I saw no reason to leave.

She had let Benz back in from the balcony, and he was draped over most of the end of the bed.

"A wonderful thing has happened to me," she said.

"Yeah. It was great for me too."

She giggled and poked me. "I just realized I no longer care that I don't have a left breast."

"I never did care."

"I know that. But despite all the things I did to change my life and my attitude, I did care. Not so much that it was an obsession. But it bothered me. And now it doesn't, thanks to you."

"Just because I don't care, you don't care?"

"Not exactly."

Shoot. I'm still clueless.

"You gave me that book you got from Ms. Po. A line in one of the poems is, 'You only lose what you cling to.' After I found you, I stopped clinging to that breast. So it's no longer lost."

She scooted closer to me. "Did you ever live with any of those girlfriends you told me about?"

"No."

"Why not?"

"I was waiting for that special someone."

Not exactly true, but I didn't want to spoil the moment by saying none of them were interested.

"Would that special someone be me?"

"You wouldn't ask if you didn't already know."

She thrust up her arms and yelled, "Yes!"

Then she rolled over on top of me and kissed me.

When my heart rate returned to normal, I said, "Not that anything could dissuade me from moving in, but are you done with your one-at-a-time list?"

She shook her head. "There's one more thing on it. And it isn't nearly as dramatic as the others. In fact, it isn't about me. It's about my father. But now is not the time. There is one thing I want to ask about."

"Which is?"

"Your relationship with Susannah."

"We're friends, Sharice. I love that girl, but not romantically. She's like a niece, a baby sister, a friend and a partner in crime all rolled into one. But she is not and never has been a girlfriend. You are *ma petite amie.*"

I got out of bed and traipsed into the living room. Why is it that *traipsed* springs to mind when we are naked?

I traipsed back and handed her a small package.

She unwrapped *The Gospel According to Coco Chanel.* "This is great."

"I couldn't afford one of her dresses, so I bought you a book about her instead."

I handed her a larger package.

She tore off the paper. "A Georgia O'Keeffe knock-off. Spectacular. I'll never be able to afford a real one, and I think prints are tacky. This will look great. I know exactly where I'll hang it."

She started to kiss me again and stopped. "Why the sneaky grin?"

"It's not a knock-off. It's a genuine O'Keeffe."

"You can't be serious."

"She didn't quite finish it. She never signed it. And it has a tear in it that you can hardly see now that it's framed. But it is a genuine O'Keeffe."

"I should have known it was real. Look at that cliff. It does more than just picture a piece of geology. It reminds you how you feel when you're in those lonely wild places."

"I guess that's what O'Keeffe meant when she said, 'I could say things with color and shapes that I couldn't say any other way—things I had no words for.'"

"I'll treasure this painting forever."

"Good, because you'll have to keep it. Its provenance is a bit dodgy."

She laughed. "Judging from the stuff in the newspaper, so is yours. I guess I'll have to keep you too."

Acknowledgments

Georgia O'Keeffe taught at West Texas State Normal College from 1916 to 1918. My tenure as the academic vice president of that institution—renamed West Texas State University—coincided with the seventy-fifth anniversary of its founding. I decided we should ask O'Keeffe to grant us the right to make prints of a painting she had done while teaching there and allow us to sell those prints to fund scholarships.

I gave the task of approaching Ms. O'Keeffe to my wife, whose charm and grace were best suited to the task. And it helped that she is also an artist and an art historian. O'Keeffe granted her request. So Georgia O'Keeffe is the first person I want to acknowledge. For helping fund scholarships, for inspiring this book and—most important—for her hauntingly beautiful paintings of New Mexico.

The second person I wish to acknowledge is my wife, Lai. For everything.

Thanks to my daughter, Claire, and my sister, Pat, for reading the manuscript. Thanks also to the non-family beta readers who could have more easily said no. That group includes Ofélia Nikolova, who not only makes excellent substantive suggestions but also catches typos in all the languages employed. She is personally acquainted with every diacritical mark and knows which way they slant. Stephanie Raffel of Sandia Park, New Mexico, read the manuscript with her usual enthusiasm, and her experience as a Spanish teacher and margarita drinker were both helpful. Tom Lake, archaeologist, is not responsible for any errors in Hubie's statements about the discipline, especially the fact that Hubie uses *shard*, which all self-respecting anthropologists know should be *sherd* or, even better, *potsherd*. Maybe Hubie uses the nonprofessional term as a jab at the program that expelled him. Even I don't completely understand him. Tom is not only an excellent archaeologist, he is also an expert on New Mexico, and most summers will find him there with his students. He allows them to take time out from doing archaeology things in order to do other things such as visit Old Town and Treasure House Books. Since most of his students are from New York, a trip to New Mexico must be an eye-opening experience.

I also benefited from the suggestions of Lisa Airey, author of the excellent *Touching the Moon*. I loved that book, even though it's in a genre I rarely read. Andy and Carolyn Anderson of Questa, New Mexico, have been with me from the start of this series and, like my other readers, are friends as well. Jane Robinson of Lake Park, Georgia, is in the group, as is newcomer Barbara M. Lane, MSW LCSW. Barb is also a Diplomate Jungian Analyst, and you can make of that what you will.

As always, I am indebted to my agent triumvirate—Barbara Bitela, Ed Silver and Philip Turner for their support and advice.

Thanks to my publisher, Open Road, for hiring the talented Peggy Hageman to edit this book. Her insight into the characters and her ability to follow the convoluted plot resulted in changes that make me appear to be an accomplished writer.

Special thanks to two friends who are, in fact, accomplished writers—Tim Hallinan and Anne Hillerman. They made time in their busy schedules to read the manuscript and write blurbs. Anne and Tim are each a source of reading enjoyment and a reminder of the miles I have to go as a writer.